NEGOTIATING LOVE

Other books by Roni Denholtz:

Lights of Love
Somebody to Love

NEGOTIATING LOVE

•

Roni Denholtz

AVALON BOOKS
NEW YORK

PRINTED IN THE UNITED STATES OF AMERICA
ON ACID-FREE PAPER
BY HADDON CRAFTSMEN, BLOOMSBURG, PENNSYLVANIA

For my mom,
Selma Rosenthal Paitchel,
who always said I could do anything if I put my mind to it;
and in loving memory of my dad,
Howard Paitchel,
who always said I was very creative.

Chapter One

"How much did you say the new tires will cost?" A mental picture of her check merrily bouncing flashed through Valerie McFadden's mind. Fighting the anxious feeling gnawing at her, she stared at the man behind the counter of Family Tire Center.

He repeated the price, then added, "Your front tires are balding. That's why you got the flat. We can show you where they're worn down. And," he continued, looking troubled, "your rear tires aren't in such good shape either. You should really replace them too, for your own safety."

Valerie swallowed, wondering how she was going to afford to replace her two front tires, let alone all four. She wouldn't get another paycheck until September 15—three weeks from now. The Board of Education paid the teachers twice a month, and they got no paychecks during the summer. And her part-time summer job at the discount store in the next town didn't give her much spending money either.

"Can I wait at least a few weeks to replace the back tires?" she asked.

The man gave her a sympathetic look. "If you're not driving long distances, you might be able to. But I wouldn't wait too long."

Valerie sighed, reviewing her finances silently. She had money budgeted for food for the next few weeks, and she'd just bought a couple of outfits for the new school year. But she hadn't anticipated getting new tires. However, she couldn't drive an unsafe car; she'd have to charge the ex-

1

pense. She was reluctant to take any money out of the savings account which she so carefully added to each month.

The young man—he couldn't be over twenty-five—was twisting his gleaming gold wedding ring. He caught her look, and grinned. "I just got married a few weeks ago," he said.

"Congratulations. Well, I guess I'll have to charge the front tires, and wait a few weeks to get new ones for the back."

"Ok," he said. "I'll tell the mechanic. It should only be about twenty minutes til your car's ready. But don't wait too long to get those other tires."

"Alright." Valerie sighed inwardly again.

"Excuse me." A deep voice from the other end of the counter broke in.

Valerie turned to see a tall, handsome man with thick brown hair and blue eyes moving closer to the young man.

As she did, she felt something leap inside her—like when she tried to skip jump-rope with a student. Her heart accelerated.

She looked from one to the other. They looked very much alike, with similar features and the exact same shade of brown hair touched with auburn. Brothers, she surmised. But the older man, who looked around thirty, had a certain air of maturity, of quiet command, that the younger man lacked. It added appeal to his handsome features.

"I couldn't help overhearing," the man was saying, a smile touching his mouth. "You know, we're running a Labor Day sale next week. If you come in and get your back tires then, you'll save fifteen percent on each tire."

"Oh! Thank you. That will be a help." Valerie tilted her head and smiled up at the man, He had to be over six feet— he was towering over her. "I'll come back then."

"Sorry, I should have mentioned it," the younger man apologized. "I was thinking about my wife . . ."

The older man offered him a tolerant look. "Daydreaming again? The sale starts next Thursday," he continued, focusing on Valerie. "Thursday and Friday it won't be as busy as Saturday, so I suggest you come in one of those days." He leaned closer, and Valerie felt her heart skip again.

"Thank you," she repeated, grateful for the suggestion. She tried to ignore her thudding heart. Labor Day wouldn't be the most convenient for her budget, but a sale would definitely save her money . . . something she tried to do whenever possible. She caught the faintest whiff of the man's masculine aftershave.

She smiled, and he smiled back.

And her heart did a little flip.

A handsome man who was also nice . . . she could just hear her sister whispering, "Go for it, girl! Ask his name!" But then, Jill was a self-admitted flirt.

Valerie looked from one man to the other. "You must be brothers," she said, deciding that might be a subtle way to ask his name.

"Cousins, actually," the younger man said, grinning. "I'll go tell Sam to replace your front tires." He disappeared through the door to the huge garage.

"Thanks," she called after him, then turned to look at his older cousin.

He was studying her.

She felt herself flushing. What did he think of her, she wondered? She was wearing denim shorts, her old sandals and a simple pink T-shirt. She knew she looked far from glamorous. But then, she hadn't expected to meet a good-looking man when she drove her limping car to the tire center that warm August morning. A man who somehow did something to her insides, making them feel like melting ice cream whenever he smiled.

For an instant they regarded each other. He leaned closer, and smiled again. Valerie wondered if he was subtly flirting with her. Then the slap of sandaled feet broke the moment, sounding above the old Beatles tune on the nearby radio.

"Look!" A young girl ran out from what must have been the office area. The top of her head was visible behind the counter, her thick, straight brown hair the same gleaming color as the hair on the man standing before her.

Of course. Valerie felt her heart dip and slowly sink: a handsome, thirty-something man like this one must be married already. And apparently a father.

The girl stretched her arms out, holding a colored picture. "I drew Riley," she said proudly. Valerie glimpsed a drawing of a dog.

"Wow! It looks just like her," the man said, his voice full of enthusiasm. "We'll have to hang it on the refrigerator."

Disappointed, Valerie forced herself to tamp down the attraction she'd been feeling. Not now, she told herself sternly. He's a married man.

She sighed once more. "Thanks again." She smiled at him, then went to sit on one of the chairs in the waiting area. Settling on the comfortable chair, she pulled the romance novel she'd been reading from her purse and opened it.

So, she'd felt an instant attraction to the man. It had happened to her once or twice. But it was obvious this guy was not available.

Someday she'd meet the right man, she reminded herself. Someday.

For a second, Stuart's face flashed across her mind. She firmly pushed it away. She wasn't going to think about Stuart's betrayal.

She was happy with her life. She loved her teaching job in western New Jersey. She liked Green Valley, the small town she taught in and now lived in too. And she had good friends she could count on. If she was just a little more financially secure, she'd be perfectly happy.

And if she could find true love . . . someday.

She began to read. But as she did, she kept seeing the book's hero as a tall man with thick brown hair and blue eyes.

Chapter Two

"Everyone ready? Let's go!" Bernie Carlisle's voice rang out.

Valerie rose with the other members of the teachers' negotiations team, feeling a rush of anticipation, nervousness and determination all rolled into one. Especially determination. She gripped her briefcase tightly as she followed Bernie, the leader of the team, out the door of the faculty room and into the high school's long corridor. The handles dug into her hand.

"Any idea who the Board will have on their team this year?" asked Phyllis, a woman in her fifties and seasoned member of the team.

"The usual bunch, I guess," Bernie answered. A tall man with snowy white hair, Bernie had been a history teacher at the high school for nearly forty years. "Plus, I heard that new board member joined their team—the young guy who replaced Jones when Jones moved. Some guy named Cooper."

"Ah, yes," Phyllis said, nodding. "His family's lived here for generations."

"I hope negotiations will go smoother this year than last time," said Al, another team member.

"Don't count on it," Valerie's friend, Anne Baroni, said.

Valerie shot Anne a look. Anne, who had been teaching at Green Valley Elementary several years longer than Valerie, had negotiated the last time around. In fact, Anne's enthusiasm was one of the factors that influenced Valerie to join the negotiations team when the call went out for volunteers.

"Time will tell," Bernie philosophized as they rounded the corner and proceeded down another hall. Reaching the door of the Board of Education conference room, the teachers filed in slowly.

The rich aroma of fresh coffee struck Valerie as she entered the carpeted room. Phyllis and Jim placed boxes of doughnuts and the paper goods they'd brought on the same table as the coffee and tea and Anne added a bowl of ready-made fruit salad.

Valerie set her worn briefcase down on one of the chairs in the middle of the long, oval-shaped table that dominated the room. Anne gave her a smile as she placed her own equally used briefcase on Valerie's right, and Phyllis slid into the seat on Valerie's left.

"You've been through this before. Do you feel comfortable?" Valerie murmured to Phyllis.

Phyllis shrugged. "This is my fourth—no, fifth—time on the team. So yes, it's comfortable, but I always hope it will go smoother than it has in the past."

"Don't worry," Anne said in a low voice to Valerie. "The first meeting is formal, just to establish negotiations. Everyone presents unrealistic demands. Not too much gets done."

"I'm not worried," Valerie said. And she wasn't. She really wanted to be on the team, to make sure the next contract was beneficial to her fellow teachers. She knew it was too early in the process to worry that things wouldn't go well. They were just starting—they would barely scratch the surface tonight, Bernie had told them earlier.

But she did want to do a good job. For her. For her coworkers.

For her father's memory.

"C'mon, let's get some of that coffee," Anne suggested.

As Valerie sat back down with her cup, the Board of Education members filed into the room. The Board President, Marvin Tyler, gave a tight-lipped smile and nodded his gray head to Bernie, who sat in the first seat. The lawyer for the Board, looking simultaneously sophisticated and bored, was right behind him. They were followed by a man and a woman who Valerie recognized as long-time board members: the elderly Secretary for the Board, Mrs. Haggerty, and another man—the one from the Tire Center!

She started. She hadn't seen him last week when she bought the back tires for her car. His cousin had been behind the counter. But the older cousin had, unfortunately, drifted through her mind several times.

He must be the new board member Bernie had mentioned! What was his name—Mr. Cooper?

He met her eyes, and she saw the instant recognition flaring there. He remembered meeting her too!

She bent her head and inhaled the comforting scent of brewed coffee, trying to recall exactly what she'd heard in the faculty room about this newly-elected board member.

Something about him being a local boy, growing up in the area. His family owned a business which he was now running since his father had retired. Of course! The Family Tire Center! And he was the youngest board member to serve in many years.

And what else? She wished she'd paid more attention to the chit chat now. Hadn't someone told her he was single, but raising a niece and nephew? She'd have to ask Bernie later.

Single . . . ?

But on top of that thought came another squashing one: true, he might be single. But the handsome and friendly Mr. Cooper was on the Board of Education. On the opposite side of the table.

Valerie blew on her coffee, cooling it, then took a quick sip. It tasted hearty and went down her throat smoothly. She looked up and found that Douglas Cooper was studying her. As her eyes rested on him, he gave her a causal, friendly smile that sent her pulse rate up.

Even seated, it was apparent he was taller than six feet.

His rich brown hair shone under the fluorescent lights, the reddish highlights gleaming. His broad shoulders were evident beneath his gray suit jacket.

She wondered, irreverently, if he was wearing the masculine aftershave he'd had on when they met. And chastised herself for the thought.

Valerie, stop it, she warned herself. *Just because a handsome man has taken the seat opposite you is no reason to ogle him.*

She deliberately switched to studying the other team members who were taking hot drinks and seating themselves across from the teachers.

They began with formal introductions. The Board President, Marvin Tyler, gave his tight-lipped smile again, and introduced the lawyer, Mr. Moore, Mrs. Haggerty, the board secretary, and the two experienced board members, Carl Warren and Brenda Zinkowski.

". . . and our newest Board member, Douglas Cooper," Marvin Tyler finished, indicating the owner of the Tire Center.

Douglas smiled at the teachers, a friendly grin, Valerie thought. He was new, young . . . perhaps he'd be understanding of the teachers' positions during the negotiations process. Maybe he'd even be an asset! she thought hopefully.

Bernie had begun introducing the members of the teachers' team. Al Cooney, Jim Sanders, Phyllis Newstein, Anne Baroni, and Valerie McFadden, "a third grade teacher at Green Valley Elementary, who's new to our team," he concluded with a smile.

There were murmurs of greeting.

"Let's get down to business," Bernie said easily, and it was evident he had done this before. "We have a proposal we've drafted for next year's contract." He removed a sheaf of papers from his briefcase.

Valerie watched as the papers were distributed. She already knew what her team's proposals were. The team members, afraid that this session would be like previous ones, had drawn up a demanding list.

Though it was only the second week of September and the first full week of school, the negotiations team had met three times since school ended in June. With the process taking many months, the teacher's team had started a year before the next contract was due.

"We, too, have a proposal," Mr. Tyler said smoothly.

Valerie glanced at Anne. Anne had described the game-playing that often went on at the start of negotiations. But she had hoped that this time things would be different. Would it?

"They always chip away at what we ask for," Phyllis had told Valerie weeks ago. "If we give them realistic demands, they'll cut them down. So we start big and hope to end with something decent." It was the usual way they worked, Anne had added.

As she was passed a copy of the board's formal-looking document, Valerie felt uneasy. Anne turned and caught her look, giving Valerie a reassuring smile. She'd been through this before. Valerie relaxed, taking the lead from her friend.

She looked down at the papers. The front page bore the title, "Proposed Agreement between the Board of Education of Green Valley and the Teachers' Association."

What a waste of paper—and tax payers' money—Valerie thought. Did they really need a separate title page? Turning to the first page, she began to skim the Board's proposal.

The first point, no pay raise, was something the Board had included in their first proposal every year since Valerie had started teaching here. No surprise there. The second point, though, caused her to start. She had to refrain from gasping.

The Board was proposing the teachers assume all their own insurance costs!

Valerie had heard of other Boards of Education in New Jersey trying this over the last few years. But so far none in this area had succeeded. It was a preposterous idea. Did they really expect the teachers to assume the cost of their own insurance? Corporate employers all over the state— not just school boards—paid for employee insurance.

Valerie fought to keep her face straight. Bernie had coached her to remain calm and poker-faced. "It's the unwritten rule," he had told her when she joined the negotiations team. "Don't let them—the board—know what you're thinking."

She glanced at the others. Phyllis wore a small frown, but otherwise the other members of their team were busy reading, their faces expressionless.

She fought an impulse to look at the handsome Mr. Douglas Cooper, and went on with her reading.

The third proposal, taking away one of the teachers' three personal days, was also insulting. Many teachers needed those days for personal business, illness in the family or deaths, or even religious holidays not covered in the usual contracts.

Valerie stopped reading and surveyed the Board members as they scanned the papers Bernie had given them. Her eyes returned to Douglas Cooper. She wanted to sigh inwardly. Her hope that Douglas Cooper, being younger than most of the Board members, might bring some sense and balance to the Board's thinking was rapidly diminishing.

Like the others, he was reading. She noticed his lips tighten in displeasure as he turned the first page. She looked at Mr. Tyler, then the lawyer—and then back to Douglas.

She wished she wasn't so conscious of his handsome face, his strong, masculine hands gripping the papers, the auburn lights in his thick brown hair that just invited her fingers to run through it . . .

Was she crazy? How could she be having these thoughts during a negotiations session—thoughts about a member of the opposing team? Valerie straightened up in her chair as she mentally scolded herself. Enough. Get your mind back on the task at hand, she ordered herself sternly.

Valerie took out her pen and scribbled a note on one of the pages of the proposal. The partial dental insurance that the teachers had fought so long for and finally succeeded in obtaining two years ago was another item the Board wanted to eliminate.

She wanted to sigh, but resisted. She knew her job as a negotiations team member was an important one. She was striving to get a good raise for her fellow teachers, better benefits and working conditions. Although teachers were now paid better than when her father started out, it was an important and often stressful job, demanding the very best a person had to give. She owed it to her coworkers to fight for job improvements.

She owed it to the memory of her father.

Valerie's first couple of years of teaching had been in a large city in New Jersey, and the small, overcrowded school had only added to the many problems her inner-city students faced. She had been thrilled to get a job in Green Valley four years ago, even though she now lived over an hour away from her family. Here, in western New Jersey, there was space to breathe. And although her students had their share of problems, it was a much safer environment, in a beautiful area.

Still, she and her coworkers often worked under less-than-perfect conditions. Even here in the country, last year she had been faced with a book, chair and desk shortage for her students, and one pupil whose severe emotional problems were not addressed by the Child Study Team until the school year was nearly over.

And even though she did like it here, the pay was less than in some of the neighboring, more affluent school districts. She would not let anything distract her from the team's purpose—getting better conditions, benefits and pay for its members. Certainly no member of the board's team was going to sway her from her purpose. She heard Bernie clear his throat. "I think we should adjourn for a few minutes," he said abruptly.

Phyllis gave a slight nod in agreement.

"I agree," the Board lawyer concurred, in his lackluster voice.

Everyone stood up. The air now held a slight chill, Valerie thought, that had nothing to do with the cool September evening weather. As they filed out, Valerie looked at the Board members.

Douglas Cooper was watching her again.

Once back in the faculty room, the teachers on the team had plenty to say.

"No raise again," Phyllis said with disgust, plopping on the worn sofa. "Aren't they getting tired of that old chestnut?"

"And taking away our medical insurance!" Valerie declared. "Don't they know what doctor and hospital costs are today even for simple things? And insurance doesn't cover it all! It's not like we make enough money to afford great medical care!"

"It's outrageous," Anne agreed, seating herself next to Phyllis.

"Unfortunately, they're not the only ones trying this," Bernie told them. He shoved his hands in his pockets. "I heard that the Board of Ed in Pine Grove made the exact same proposal yesterday to their teachers."

"The state Board of Ed is probably advising everyone to try that," said Al gloomily. In his late forties, he was the vice-president of the teachers' union.

"Our members will have a fit," Jim, a teacher in his thirties, added.

They all complained loudly for a minute until Bernie held up his hand. "Look, let's not get carried away," he said. "We know how our board is. They play games. They know they won't get away with this, but they figure they'll throw it in the mix to distract us from the issue of money . . . or maybe as another point they can back down from later."

The temerity of the board's suggestion was causing them

to all feel on edge. Valerie could sense the anxiety in the air. She met Anne's eyes, who raised her own in return. Valerie realized she had slipped into her old habit of nibbling on her pen. She forced herself to stop. She thought she'd given that up ages ago.

It might be her first time with the team, but she shouldn't let the board's ridiculous proposal get her down. She made a conscious effort to relax.

Both Jim and Al were pacing around the room now.

"What do *you* think?" Bernie asked Valerie suddenly.

"I think their suggestions are preposterous!" Valerie said hotly.

"We better not come on too strong just yet," Phyllis cautioned. "It's only the first night of negotiations."

"I agree." Bernie nodded. "I vote we simply state that we're sticking to our demands."

"Yes," Anne said. "Then we'll throw the ball in their court. And see what they say."

"Nothing, probably," Al muttered. "This doesn't look good for this year's negotiations."

"Now, don't be too pessimistic," Phyllis chided. "You know they pull this kind of thing all the time."

"All agreed?" Bernie asked. At their nods, he finished, "Okay, let's go back in."

The team members stood up. Valerie glanced at Anne for her reaction. Anne was frowning. This was *not* going well. Valerie knew Anne had expected the usual formalities tonight. But it seemed that Anne was now becoming pessimistic about the way things were going.

The board conference room was empty when they entered. The board members had not returned from their offices, so the teachers scattered. Bernie and Al walked down the hall, while Phyllis went to pour herself more coffee. Jim sat rereading the board's proposal.

"Do you want some coffee?" Anne asked Valerie.

"No," Valerie answered. "I think I've had enough. I'm feeling fidgety."

"It's just because it's your first time on the team," Anne said.

"And because it's not off to a good start," Valerie pointed out.

Anne sighed. "Yeah."

Her friend's agreement made Valerie feel worse. "Maybe I'll take a walk," she said.

"Okay," Anne said. "I want to read over their proposal again."

Valerie left the room. Bernie and Al had gone down the corridor to their left, so Valerie turned right, wanting to be alone with her thoughts. The heels of her plain black pumps tapped musically against the newly-cleaned tile floor as she walked rapidly down the long stretch of hall.

Douglas Cooper stood up and stretched his long legs.

The teachers' proposals were ridiculous. A 20% raise over two years? What, were they kidding? The taxpayers could never afford that! The school budget had barely squeaked by this year. With the distinct possibility that they would have to have a referendum to add on to the three elementary schools in the near future, what with the town's population growing, it was going to be touch and go as to how many other things could be included in the next budget. And they had asked for dental insurance for the whole family—another ridiculous request. Plus, a better prescription plan—the one the teachers had right now was good enough! Better, in fact, than the one he and his cousin Sean had as business owners.

"I want to make a call," Carl Warren said, and left the room.

"I think I'll go for a walk," Douglas told the others. The board's team had decided not to rush back to the conference room, despite their unanimous agreement that they were not going to move on their proposals.

Douglas strode down the corridor. He found his mind

wandering back to thoughts of the attractive young woman, Valerie McFadden, who he'd first met at Family Tire.

She had turned out to be a teacher, of all things!

He'd been attracted to her from the start. She was cute, with a beautiful face and lovely dark eyes. And she'd seemed warm and friendly, once she got over the idea that her car was going to cost more money than she'd anticipated.

He had thought of her several times during the last few weeks, and had even been tempted to look up her phone number on the Family Tire forms to call her, maybe suggest going out for a cup of coffee, or dinner. Then he'd thought maybe he'd talk to her again when she brought her car back. But she'd returned when Sean was there, and he was out with Matthew and Lindsay, buying their school supplies.

He shook his head. She was a teacher . . . and this group of teachers seemed especially demanding.

The last thing he needed was a demanding woman who was obsessed over money.

It was his first term on the school board. Concern for future education plans in the town, now that he was raising his nephew and niece, had prompted him to run for the Board of Education last spring. The other members of the board then urged him to join the board's negotiating team, pleading that they needed a fresh voice among the experienced members.

So here he was, ready to do his part to make sure Green Valley had excellent schools . . . and that the tax payers were not stretched too tight to insure it.

He grimaced: the teachers' requests were out of line. The only reasonable request that he could see was for an extra bereavement day in the case of the death of a grandparent. They already had three days per occurrence in the case of a death in the immediate family . . . but Douglas knew only too well that was not enough.

It had been only a little over a year since he'd lost his own brother. Keith and his wife Denise had been on their way back from an evening at the movies, when their car had been hit head on by a speeding drunk driver. Neither had survived. They had left Matthew and Lindsay orphaned. Since Denise's family lived on the west coast and the children hardly knew them, it had been logical for Keith and Denise to name Douglas as the children's guardian in their wills.

Douglas had had to deal with his own grief at the deaths of his brother and sister-in-law, while dealing with the pain and fright of their sweet kids. It had been a very difficult time for them all. His parents and aunt and uncle had flown up from Florida, but they were really not young enough to deal with two children, and Douglas knew in his heart he was the logical person to raise them.

His cousin and business partner, Sean, had helped of course. But Sean and Jessica weren't even married at the time. Jessica was still finishing college.

Douglas was grateful now that Sean and his new wife could help out with babysitting when he had to work late or go to Board meetings. They truly loved Matthew and Lindsay.

Sean and Jessica had even urged him to get out and start dating again—something he just hadn't had time to do since adopting the children. He knew the children needed him, needed someone to care for them and help them get through the tragic loss of both parents. He'd pushed his own need to socialize aside, spending as much time as possible with them.

Douglas walked briskly, feeling the need to move around, to get some exercise. He usually worked out at home two or three times a week, but today he'd been too busy.

He'd been thinking that perhaps he should start going out again. After all, a well-rounded person got out sometimes with friends. He needed to resume his own activities, just as the children had gotten back to soccer games and dance lessons.

Why did Valerie McFadden's face pop into his mind precisely at that moment?

He'd been attracted to her from the moment he'd seen her at Family Tire. And who wouldn't be? She was slender, petite, with a gorgeous face. Long curly black hair and a friendly smile enhanced her appeal.

How could someone so pretty and friendly come up with the ridiculous demands the teachers were making? Was she intelligent? Shrewd or naïve? He didn't know.

But he had a strong desire to find out.

The hall here was brightly lit, and he could smell a strong disinfectant. Passing the cafeteria, he heard two janitors inside, sweeping brooms across the floor, while a small radio on a table played a popular rock song by Santana.

He felt restless, and suspected it was not merely his lack of exercise today that was causing it. He had a feeling it was because of a certain petite brunette with a sunny smile. He turned the corner, and started walking up another hall. This one was in shadows. His steps slowed as he peered down the dim corridor.

There was something mysterious, he thought, about a school at night. Shadows curled near closed classroom doors. The halls were nearly silent, the only noises faint and far away. A far cry from the usually crowded, noisy state of things.

He heard a steady tap from ahead of him and paused. Footsteps, he realized, coming closer. Short, feminine footfalls. The *tap-tap-tap* got closer, and from the shadows, a shape emerge: Valerie McFadden.

"Hi," he said.

She gasped. "Oh! You—you startled me."

"I'm sorry, I didn't mean to," he said, drawing closer.

For some reason, his pulse was accelerating. He must

have been startled too, he concluded. Here he was in a quiet
place, thinking it was mysterious—and a beautiful woman
had stepped into his path . . .

"The school can be kind of spooky at night," she said,
almost echoing his thoughts.

"Yeah."

"I want to thank you again," she said in a rush, "for
helping me out. I didn't expect to need four new tires—
and I appreciate your telling me about the sale. I need to
save money whenever I can."

"No problem." He paused. "How's the car driving now?"

"Oh fine. I mean, it's not a new car, but it's good and
dependable—and at least I know I have safe tires." She
flashed a smile.

Standing so close, Douglas was acutely conscious of how
small Valerie was compared to him. He caught the faintest
trace of something floral: her cologne. It was subtle and
feminine. But she looked all business in her dark red suit.
She was a teacher. On the negotiations team. Yet she appeared to be pretty young. He asked, "Have you been teaching long?"

"I've taught at Green Valley Elementary for four years,"
she said, her tone proud. "Before that, I taught for several
years in Jersey City. But I wanted to move out to the country," she said. "I really like this area."

If she had been teaching about six years, Douglas cal-
culated that she must be twenty-eight—although she looked
younger. Her face was youthful.

"The area is nice. I've lived here all my life," he said,
wanting to keep the conversation going. She might be on
the teachers' team, but he was intensely curious about her,
and wanted to take this unexpected opportunity to talk.

"It is nice," she agreed. "I grew up in Union, and it's
much more crowded in that area of the state." She shifted
her position slightly, looking a little stiff. Douglas wondered if she felt uncomfortable talking to him in the darkened hallway.

"I grew up here," he repeated, leaning against the row of lockers. "I went to high school right in this building."

"I guess you liked the auto mechanics classes," she said.

He laughed. "They were easy for me. My dad and my uncle owned our business when I was young, and I kind of grew up around cars and trucks. But I took business classes, too, and majored in business in college."

"I always liked the English and music classes in high school," Valerie said. Did he imagine it, or was she relaxing just a little? "And, of course, history."

"Of course?" he prompted.

"My father was a history teacher." It came out curtly, and Douglas saw her expression change. She looked . . . sad.

"Was?" he asked. "Did he retire?"

"No. He passed away." Her voice caught. She turned her head, looking to the side.

Her voice was low, and standing so close, Douglas had to fight an urge to touch her reassuringly. "I'm sorry," he said. He thrust his hands in his pockets.

"I miss him a lot," she said, her voice still low. She turned back to regard Douglas.

In that moment, he felt a strong comradeship for Valerie McFadden. They had experienced similar losses. He wished he could offer some comfort, put a hand on her shoulder, *something*. "I know how hard it is. I lost my older brother and sister-in-law a little over a year ago. It's difficult, isn't it?"

She nodded, and he thought she might be fighting back tears.

She looked so small, so feminine, and he had to steel himself from giving her a soothing, friendly hug. Had they been at Family Tire, he might have done that. But here, in the school where they were negotiating, it would have been inappropriate.

"I'm sorry for your loss too," she said, her voice gentle.

Again he caught a hint of a light floral fragrance. And

his pulse rate seemed to increase. Being so close to Valerie was having a strange effect on him. Every inch of him seemed to be humming like a new car motor. He'd better start doing some socializing, he decided. He couldn't remember the last time a woman had had such a profound effect on him. Sure, Valerie was beautiful, but he'd met beautiful women before. Maybe it was because Valerie seemed to be such a warm person?

Or maybe it simply was his lack of female companionship during this last year. A lack that was highly unusual for him. All he knew was that he was feeling totally aware right now, more alive than he had since . . . well, since Keith died.

And he itched to reach out and give Valerie some comfort too.

He took a deep breath, fighting the impulse. "Has it been long since your father passed away?"

"A couple of years." He guessed from her voice that she still had tears in her eyes, although he couldn't see them in the dim hall.

He leaned closer, until they were only inches apart.

Valerie tilted her head up and gazed at him.

What on earth was she doing? Valerie thought. Standing here, so close to this handsome, sympathetic man, Valerie had almost forgotten just who Douglas Cooper was. Never mind that since the moment she'd met him in the hall she'd felt electrical sparks springing through her—and suspected he felt them too. She had the craziest impulse to reach out and stroke his cheek. To offer comfort.

Or was she imagining that he felt something too? Were the sparks only on her side? The important thing was, she was feeling them. And she didn't want to, not for Douglas Cooper, a member of the Board of Education!

She fought to get control of the excitement that pumped through her. No, no, no. She took a deep breath. "I have to get back to the meeting room," she blurted out.

And just as she said it, she heard Anne's voice faintly from the other end of the hall: "Valerie?"

She tried to smile at Douglas, but knew it must have looked stiff. "I am sorry for your loss," she repeated. "It must be very tough to lose a sibling, someone who's so young."

"Yes." His voice was solemn.

"Well, I guess I'll see you soon," she said. Oh dear, she sounded like an awkward teenager. She moved back. "Bye."

Turning on her heel, she hurried down the hall, hearing Douglas' smooth, "See you later," behind her.

She reached the main hall, and the brighter light seemed intense. "I'm here, Anne," she called.

As she walked, she sighed. She was attracted to Douglas Cooper. How ironic! She realized now that he wasn't married—he must be raising his brother's children, and the little girl she'd seen at Family Tire was his niece. But he was a Board of Ed member, which made him out of reach. Why did she have to feel this attraction, feel this intense pull, to him of all people?

She paused, fighting to control her breathing, which she was sure was more rapid than usual. She was Valerie McFadden, teacher and member of the teachers' negotiating team. She was a professional. She was here for a purpose: to fight for a fair contract. No one was going to shake her from that goal. Not even the masculine, mesmerizing Douglas Cooper.

Slowly, she rounded the next corner. Anne was striding down the hall.

"Where were you?" her friend asked.

"I just went for a walk," Valerie said. "I guess I went a little farther than I intended to. Are we starting?"

"I think we're about to," Anne said. She gave Valerie a long look. "Are you alright?"

"I was just thinking about my dad," Valerie said hastily.

Anne nodded. "I know, you think of him often." Anne's voice softened. "But at least you still have your Mom, and your sister and brother."

"True," Valerie agreed.

They walked in companionable silence together, arriving at the board conference room just ahead of the board members.

Valerie couldn't help looking at Douglas when he entered. He quirked an eyebrow at her, and she gave him a smile which she suspected looked stiff.

Mr. Tyler began at once. "After much consideration," he said, and went on to mention the board's concern with rising costs, irate taxpayers, and numerous fringe topics, such as the national unemployment rate.

As he droned on, Valerie looked at each board member. They wore carefully neutral expressions. All, except, for Douglas. As he caught her eye he smiled slowly.

Valerie felt a wave of warmth slowly creep through her. Uh oh, she thought. One smile from Douglas Cooper and her body temperature rose? She should not be reacting this way. Her fingers tightened on her pen. Mr. Tyler finished his long-winded speech. He could have said it in two minutes, she thought. The gist of it was, the board was not making any concessions.

Bernie then launched into a similar, but shorter, speech. Costs were rising, and teachers' salaries weren't even keeping up with inflation. Not like salaries in the corporate world. Working conditions were tough, teachers were getting larger classes, students who couldn't speak English, more special education pupils put back into the mainstream, state and federal services were shrinking. Teachers were ending up with extra duties and more mandated paperwork than ever before.

Valerie agreed wholeheartedly with every point Bernie made. They were overworked and underpaid, as Anne often said. Anne had it especially hard. She was a single mom, divorced with one child. But most teachers were struggling.

Jim had a wife who was at home, and two young kids. Phyllis and her husband had two out of their three kids in college.

Even Valerie was finding it a struggle, and always took a job during the summer break at a discount store in the next town. It was no wonder her father . . . At the thought of her father, Valerie's fingers pressed the pen so hard it suddenly flew across the table, landing between Douglas and Mr. Warren. Bernie paused and everyone turned to look at her.

Her cheeks grew hot. "I'm sorry," she said.

Douglas retrieved the pen, then leaned over to return it to her. His smile was casually friendly.

Valerie's insides felt like the scattered pieces of a puzzle. Douglas Cooper was one of the representatives of the Board of Ed, the same people she was up against. Judging by his stylish suit and expensive-looking briefcase, he had money and power—the very things the teachers didn't have. Yet he looked kind. How could he be such a contradiction? And why was she thinking about him so much?

Bernie was summing up his points. "So, at this time, we see no reason to change our requests." His statement was met by silence.

Valerie studied the board members' faces. They all looked impassive. When her eyes reached Douglas, he seemed to sense her look, because he turned from staring at Bernie and focused on her.

The lawyer spoke. "Perhaps we should adjourn again."

The teachers agreed, and returned to the faculty room.

Valerie found herself pacing restlessly. Anne shot her a look, then whispered, "Are you okay?"

"Yes. Just tired. I need a good night's sleep."

"Me too." Anne sighed.

Valerie knew that Anne got up even earlier than Valerie did, to get ready for work before she woke her nine-year-old son and got him ready to go to her neighbor's before school.

Al spoke up suddenly. "I think we should call in an assistant from NJEA." That was the New Jersey Education Association, and Valerie knew they had specialists, experienced negotiators with extra training who assisted local negotiating teams when things got rough.

"It's too early in the game to do that," Bernie said, shaking his head. His thick white hair waved wildly. "We don't want to look like we're upset this soon."

"I agree," Phyllis stated. "Let's play along with them a bit longer."

"I think the best thing at this point is to set up another meeting in a week or two," Bernie continued. "We'll meet before then, and see if we can make some slight—and I emphasize slight—concessions to our demands. We'll try to show that we're doing our part and we're anxious for a peaceful settlement."

Everyone wearily agreed. It was getting late, and they all had to be up early for work.

They returned to the boardroom. Bernie suggested in an amiable voice that they both read over each others' requests, and meet at the table again in a week. Mr. Tyler agreed.

Personal calendars were whipped out as they searched for a convenient date. The first one Bernie proposed was good for everyone but the board lawyer.

As they puzzled over dates, suggesting and rejecting several, Valerie looked at the calendars each person held. Jim and Bernie were using the school calendar, as was Mr. Tyler. Anne's calendar was a large one with lots of notes scrawled in. Valerie, Phyllis and Al had smaller but efficient looking calendars.

By contrast, Valerie noticed that the lawyer, Mr. Warren, Mrs. Zinkowski and Douglas Cooper had hand-held personal electronic devices. And Mrs. Haggerty sported an expensive leather-bound calendar. It was just another reminder of the differences between the teachers and the Board of Ed members, Valerie thought.

Bernie and Marvin Tyler shook hands formally, but without any real warmth. This was the signal for the others to stand up, apparently, and Valerie rose with the rest of the team members.

She felt drained, and anxious to get home. She wanted to put her feet up, play with her cats for a while and try to gather her scattered jigsaw thoughts. She left the building with her coworkers.

The night air was cool and felt good against her warm cheeks. The air was cleaner, and the sky clearer here than where she'd grown up. With a strong hint of autumn crispness in the air, it was a perfect September night.

Fall, her favorite time of year. Full of promise of the new school year, alive with beauty, and with the enticement of the holidays ahead, she loved this season the best. She paused, breathing deeply for a moment.

She said goodnight to the others and then stepped briskly to her car, feeling renewed by the refreshing air. A red jeep was parked on the side of her small car, and Valerie wondered if it belonged to a board member. She drew closer, spotting someone opening the door.

"Good night, Ms. McFadden." Douglas's voice startled her. He paused, and in the dim light of the parking lot she couldn't make out his features. But he sounded friendly.

Standing so close, Valerie couldn't suppress the memory of their encounter earlier in the hall. The memory of the tingling she'd felt when he leaned closer.

But staring her in the face was one more sign of his position: an expensive car.

"Goodnight, Mr. Cooper." She kept her voice formal. Getting into her car, she started it, flicked on the radio, and drove away, wondering about the growing attraction she felt for the man in her rearview mirror.

Chapter Three

"**B**ut Miz McFadden!" Dustin, a skinny brown-haired boy, looked up at Valerie, frustration evident on his face. "I don't get it."

Valerie moved swiftly beside Dustin's desk. As the rest of the class began their math work, she repeated the explanation she had given only a few minutes before.

"See this sign, Dustin?" She pointed to the sign in his math workbook. "This means *less than*. Eight is less than ten." She moved her finger. "This other symbol means *greater than*. Ten is greater than eight."

The boy frowned. "But how can I tell which is which? They look the same!"

Patiently, Valerie went over the lesson she had taught not ten minutes earlier. "The less than sign starts out little and gets bigger. The greater than sign starts out large and gets smaller."

She showed him a few more examples, writing on scrap paper on his desk so he could see it clearly. Then she said, "Do you remember the trick I showed everyone to help them remember?"

He shook his head. Poor Dustin, she thought. She suspected he might have a learning disability because he often reversed letters and numbers. While that was common and not cause for alarm in a first grader, by third grade the students shouldn't be doing that, at least not frequently. Plus, he had a lot of trouble paying attention in class and promptly forgot things.

"The pointy end of the symbol is always next to the smaller number," she explained again. "See? Five is *less than* twelve. The point is right there, next to the five. Kind of like the pointy end of an arrow."

She watched Dustin's face as she gave a few more examples. Suddenly his frown cleared up. "Oh! I get it. It points to the smaller number," he said cheerfully.

"Right!" Valerie applauded. "Now take a look at these numbers. One and three. Can you draw the symbol?"

She observed as Dustin carefully drew the less than symbol.

"Very good!" she praised. "One is less than three. Now try the next three and I'll check them before you go on." She stepped back, hoping he would be able to work on his own now. She glanced around to see if anyone else was in need of help, but the rest of her class was working on the problems by themselves.

She walked slowly, checking over the shoulders of a few students. It looked like everyone understood the lesson. She returned to Dustin to review the problems he'd just done, and after checking them, praised him once more and told him to continue. As she did, she heard a stirring near the door, and looked up to see a few students pointing.

"Miss McFadden!" Amanda said.

Valerie swiveled until she could get a good view of the door. Mr. Hart, the Superintendent of Schools, stood in the doorway. This must be one of his start-of-the-school-year visits, she thought. He didn't usually stop in every class—just random ones.

"Good morning," Valerie said cheerfully.

"Good morning, Miss McFadden," he said somewhat formally, but with his congenial smile. Bill Hart was tall and white haired, a dedicated administrator who had been involved in education for decades. He was considered truly fair by both the teachers and school administrators alike.

"This is Mr. Hart, the Superintendent of Schools," she

introduced him to her class. "He's kind of like the boss. Let's say good morning to Mr. Hart."

The class said in unison with her, "Good morning, Mr. Hart."

"Good morning boys and girls," he replied solemnly.

"Please continue with your work," Valerie told her pupils as she approached the door.

The children bent over their papers again, except for one girl who was eyeing the door with great curiosity. Valerie could hear more adult voices in the hall behind the superintendent.

"I'm taking some of our board members on a tour of the schools this morning," Mr. Hart said.

At his words, Valerie felt her heart start to pump harder. She wasn't nervous because an administrator was visiting her class—but board members? Which board members?

Normally the board members walked through the building, looking things over in a superficial way, more concerned with the physical aspects of the building than what was going on in the classrooms. But Valerie sensed that this time might be different.

She peered at the doorway.

Douglas Cooper walked through it.

A flare went off inside of her. But whether it was from excitement or danger, she wasn't sure.

Douglas was followed by Mrs. Zinkowski and Mr. Kelly, a man who was a long-time board member but not on the negotiations team. Mr. Hart introduced them to her, and Valerie said hello.

Douglas met her eyes with his blue ones. Instantly, he smiled. "Good morning, Ms. McFadden," he said.

He was as handsome as she remembered—maybe even more so. In the bright fluorescent lights of the classroom, his thick brown hair shone with reddish highlights. His muscular shoulders were evident beneath his simple striped shirt, which was casually open at the collar. He wore nice slacks but the whole effect was business casual—and masculine.

"Good morning." Valerie smiled at each board member in turn. Mr. Kelly nodded absently, and Mrs. Zinkowski gave her a rather haughty smile.

Somehow Valerie managed to keep her voice calm. But she was conscious that her heart was beating faster than usual. It's not often three board members came to her classroom, she told herself. Who are you kidding? A little voice within her asked. It's not often a handsome guy comes to your classroom door!

"Miss McFadden teaches third grade," Mr. Hart was saying to them. "She's one of our very creative teachers."

"Thank you," Valerie murmured.

She had tried to put Douglas Cooper out of her mind since Tuesday night's board meeting. But she'd been unsuccessful. She'd never dreamed she'd see him again so soon. She hadn't had this kind of intense reaction to a man in—well, she couldn't remember when. Even Stuart had never elicited this strong a response in her.

Mr. Hart was saying something about continuing his tour, and he hoped that she would have a good school year. She snapped back to reality in time to thank him for stopping by.

"Now the next classroom down is another third grade . . ." he said, resuming his tour.

With formal smiles, Mrs. Zinkowski and Mr. Kelly followed the superintendent.

Douglas Cooper lingered.

"That was an interesting meeting the other night," he said in a low voice.

"Interesting . . . yes," Valerie said. But the adjective "frustrating" was the one that came to mind.

Frustrating in more ways than one.

She glanced back to see that her students were still busy with their math assignment: she knew within a few minutes some of them would be finishing up.

"Perhaps we can discuss it over a cup of coffee?" he asked. "Maybe on Friday?"

Something ricocheted in Valerie, down to her toes.

Douglas Cooper wanted to see her! She couldn't help the pleasure she was feeling. At the same time, she knew it was an awkward situation to put herself in. *If only I could*, she found herself thinking. But no matter how much she wanted to, she felt funny about saying yes. Douglas was on the opposing team, after all. He stood for power and privilege.

"I don't think that would be a good idea," she said. She smiled to soften her words, but it came out wistful instead.

He leaned closer. "Why not try it and see?" There was a challenge to his tone. And possibly just a spark of humor. Her conflicting emotions were leaving Valerie at a loss for words—something unusual for her.

"Miss McFadden!" A whining voice by her side had her turning to look down at Kayla, one of her students.

She saw tears in the girl's eyes. "Yes?" She asked gently.

"Scarlett called me a hen!" Kayla tattled.

Valerie gave a silent sigh. Scarlett was a new student to the district, outspoken and sometimes mean, who came from the one small section of town boasting a dozen large, custom-built homes. This was not the first time Scarlett had picked on Kayla. Kayla, who was chunky for her age, was especially sensitive right now because her mother had informed Valerie that Kayla's parents had just separated a few weeks ago.

"Excuse me," Valerie murmured to Douglas. She bent down to Kayla's level. "That was a mean thing to do. I know you must feel bad. I'm going to speak with Scarlett right now. Go ahead back to work."

Kayla nodded, still tearful, and returned to her desk.

Valerie marched up to Scarlett's desk.

Scarlett sat there, a too-innocent expression on her face.

"Scarlett," Valerie stated, her voice low but no-nonsense.

"We went over the classroom rules the first day of class. Do you remember?"

The pretty blond girl nodded.

"And one of the rules here is, there will be *no* name-calling in my class. Do you understand that?"

Scarlett nodded again.

Valerie stared her right in the eye. Scarlett dropped her eyes, looking at her paper, and began to twist her pencil in her fingers. "I do not want that happening again," Valerie said firmly.

Scarlett shrugged, but she continued to look down. Valerie left it at that, not making threats, but leaving it up to Scarlett to wonder what would happen if she broke the rules again.

Valerie straightened and returned to Douglas, smiling and winking as she passed by Kayla's desk. Kayla gave her a shy smile.

She heard the turning of paper, the scratch of pencils writing as she neared Douglas. Taking a deep breath, she crossed her arms when she positioned herself at the doorway, as if she could put up a physical barricade against the attraction she felt towards him. It was a relief to remember that she was busy on Friday.

"No, I can't on Friday," she said. "I already have plans."

He raised his eyebrows as if questioning her schedule. "Alright. But we will see each other again, soon." His voice was strong, definitive.

He stepped back, and continued, "Thanks for letting me see your classroom. I like the way you handle your students. Now I'd better resume the tour."

Valerie thought for a moment that she heard a note of reluctance in his voice. Or had she imagined that?

"You're welcome, Mr. Cooper," she said formally.

His grinned widened. Could he possibly know how conflicted she felt? Valerie wondered.

It unnerved her.

For a second they stared at each other, and Valerie felt the magnetism in the air. She wasn't imagining it. She felt pulled towards this man—and she was willing to bet he felt something similar. She took a step backwards, breaking the charged contact. "Bye."

"Bye," he said, and turned to walk down the hall.

Valerie turned back to her class. Two of the brightest girls in the class were laying down their pencils, already finished with their work.

Her heart was still thumping hard.

Her class would be going to gym in a few minutes, and she was glad. She needed some time alone, a few minutes to collect herself. And to get her mind off the good-looking Douglas Cooper.

He'd said they'd see each other again, soon.

She was already looking forward to it.

Douglas continued the tour, but he found his mind wandering, and had trouble concentrating on what Bill Hart was saying. Instead, the pretty, feminine face of Valerie Mc-Fadden seemed to dance before his eyes.

This tour with the Superintendent of Schools was a formality board members went through at the start of each school year. He had thought little about it—until Tuesday night's negotiating session. After that, he'd looked forward to the tour, and had specifically asked Bill Hart to show the board members the classrooms of teachers on the negotiations team.

He hadn't been totally prepared for the jolt he got when he saw Valerie. In a simple, long denim jumper and white shirt, she looked modest but very appealing. Her slender figure was apparent even under the straight jumper, and her sunny smile lit up her beautiful face.

But her good looks didn't totally explain the zing of electricity he felt when he was near her. No, it was something more than that. Something intriguing and unexplainable. Attraction, his mind insisted. Pure physical attraction. That's all it is.

Watching her with her class, and interacting with the girls who had a problem, he got the impression she was firm but fair. And he had the nagging suspicion that what he was feeling for Valerie went beyond simple physical attraction.

They concluded their tour in the faculty room, where the school's principal had put out fresh doughnuts, bagels and bottles of water.

There was a large coffee pot on a side table, with a sign above it. The sign read "Coffee, 25 cents a cup, or see Marie Durning to join the coffee club!" in red marker. Douglas groped for a quarter in his pocket and then placed it in an old, ceramic dish sitting beside the coffee pot. He helped himself to the fresh coffee, milk and sugar.

There were a few teachers on preparation breaks sitting around the large rectangular table, and it seemed to him that several of them eyed the board members with suspicion. One man, correcting papers, barely even looked up.

Douglas wandered around the room as Bill Hart chatted with a couple of the teachers. The room held somebody's old couch that had rips taped with green electrical tape and a couple of assorted lounge chairs in addition to the large table and its chairs. There was a refrigerator and a small, new-looking microwave. A few posters with funny sayings were scattered on the walls, notices about the New Jersey Education Association's annual convention in November, and a big oaktag poster next to the door.

"DON'T FORGET!" it proclaimed in large block letters. "FRIDAY AFTERNOON'S FIRST DISTRICT-WIDE HAPPY HOUR!" The words happy hour were written in red marker. "CASH BAR AND FREE HORS D'OUVRES. SEE YOU AT GIANELLI'S RESTAURANT AFTER SCHOOL!" The notice concluded in small letters: "Sponsored by the Green Valley Education Association Social Committee."

Friday—the day that Valerie was busy. Now Douglas knew exactly what she would be busy with. He turned back to the teachers sitting around the table. "Can anyone go to that happy hour?" he asked casually.

One of the teachers, a man in his early thirties, looked surprised but answered readily. "Yes. The principal at the middle school goes to these things all the time."

"He usually buys a round of drinks," a blond young woman next to the man said.

"Thanks," Douglas said. He sipped his coffee.

When the board members left the room a few minutes later to go to the last elementary school on their agenda, his step was light and easy.

Valerie put aside the last spelling test. She had stayed to complete her grading work. Now all of the day's work was corrected and recorded in her grade book, and she was free to enjoy the entire weekend, with her lesson plans completed as well.

She rose and stretched. A glance at her clock told her it was four fifteen—later than she'd thought. But at least she had finished all her work.

She locked up her classroom. The school seemed unusually quiet, her heels clicking against the linoleum floor as she walked down the corridor. This afternoon the school had emptied faster than usual, even for a Friday. People were not only anxious to start the weekend, they were looking forward to the district happy hour. The first one of the school year was always the biggest and best. Though Valerie's building had already had a party for the staff, this was the first one for the whole school district of Green Valley.

She entered the school's main office, where only one secretary was present.

"Are you going to the party?" Valerie asked her as she hung her keys up on the big board.

Mrs. Avery nodded her gray head. "As soon as I finish this last letter."

"I'll see you there," Valerie said, and exited the office.

The day had turned gray with the promise of rain and the temperature had dropped in the last few hours. In her sweater and slim skirt, she shivered. Valerie hadn't bothered with a jacket this morning since it had seemed warm. She should have listened to the weather forecast, she thought, hurrying to her car.

The restaurant was only a mile from the school but since she was arriving late, Valerie found the parking lot packed. She finally found a spot two blocks away.

Once inside the restaurant she paused, letting her eyes adjust to the dim light. Then she moved forward slowly, looking for Anne and some of her other friends. The atmosphere was thick with a multitude of voices, laughter and the clink of ice in glasses. She could smell something spicy—one of the appetizers, she surmised—and soft rock music poured out from the sound system.

She stopped to greet a couple of teachers she knew from one of the other elementary schools, then continued on, scanning the crowd for her friends.

She spotted Anne at a small table. Her fair head was bending towards the head of a dark-haired man who sat with her.

The noise level here in the middle of the room was loud. Valerie circumvented several tables and said, "Hi!" when she reached Anne's.

"Oh! Valerie, hi!" Anne declared brightly. "I was wondering when you'd get here." Anne's smile was wide and her blue eyes sparkled. "Pull up a chair—if you can find one."

Her friend's tone was especially happy, and Valerie knew something was up. She grabbed an empty chair from the table beside Anne's, where several older women were sitting.

"This is Tony," Anne introduced the man beside her. "Tony Maselli. He's the new chemistry teacher at the high school." There was no mistaking the warmth in Anne's voice.

The man was dark and good-looking, and Valerie guessed he was a little younger than Anne, who was thirty-three. She smiled at both of them. "Welcome, Tony. How do you like it here so far?"

"Nice to meet you," he said, and began speaking about the advantages of their school district compared to the school system where he'd taught previously down in the southernmost portion of the state. As he talked, Valerie paused to order a Screwdriver and to try one of the stuffed mushrooms from a platter held by a waitress.

Anne was listening eagerly to Tony. Valerie watched them. Apparently the two had just met and hit it off right away. Valerie bit into the mushroom, which was stuffed with a tasty blend of crabmeat and spices. She'd stay a few minutes, she decided, then give them some time alone.

She finished her mushroom and sipped the drink the waitress brought her, as they all talked. Then, smiling, Valerie said she wanted to speak to a couple of other people and left Anne with Tony.

"Hi, Valerie," Al greeted her as she made her way through the throng. "What a session the other night!"

"It sounds like the board is using the same old tricks," Valerie said.

"Yes, but this time it's worse. Trying to make us pay for our insurance—" Al shook his head, a disgusted expression on his face.

Bernie joined them. "Hi."

"How are things going at the high school?" Valerie asked him.

"Fine, just fine. It's nice to get together for reasons other than business," he said. "I see Anne's met our new chemistry teacher. We signed him up for the union the first day of school."

"Good," Al said approvingly.

Valerie glanced back at Anne. Once again she and Tony had their heads bent close.

She hoped Anne would go out with Tony. Anne had been divorced for several years, and her husband saw their son infrequently, so Anne didn't get out much. She deserved some fun and friendship, Valerie thought.

You do too! a voice said from the back of Valerie's mind. And maybe she did, Valerie acknowledged. Not that she hadn't dated—she had. She had had several boyfriends through high school and college. Then, about a year after graduating, she'd met Stuart at a friend's house.

Stuart was a stockbroker who was handsome and fun and smart. Valerie had fallen for him—and he'd seemed to feel the same. In fact, he had said he loved her a number of times.

But his idea of love and Valerie's had been very different. Valerie's idea of love had been true, lasting love, followed by marriage and a family.

Stuart's idea was falling in love alright. But he wanted to wait for marriage and a family—maybe forever. He wanted to have a good time, live a carefree life, not be tied down. He expected to fall in and out of love many times, he'd told her. Maybe because, he revealed, his parents had married very young and always resented it. They'd ended up divorced, and both had declared it was a mistake to get tied down. He simply didn't see his romance with Valerie as lasting or leading anywhere.

"We'll enjoy it while it lasts," Stuart had said in the restaurant the last time they went out. "Then, when it ends, we'll go our separate ways."

"While it lasts?" Valerie had shot back at him. "It's ending now. I want marriage and a family. I don't want to be strung along until you get tired of me and go on to someone else."

"Too bad, babe," he'd declared. "We could have had a lot of fun for months—maybe even years."

"Not with me." She'd stood up. "I'd rather end it now then go on, knowing this relationship is going nowhere."

Stuart had shrugged. "Suit yourself."

Angry and heartbroken, Valerie had called a friend for a ride home. She hadn't wanted to spend another minute with Stuart. And she never saw him again.

Live music started up, and Valerie shook off the painful memory of Stuart's selfishness. She would never cling to a relationship that was going nowhere, even if it meant there were times when she had no boyfriend and no prospects.

One of the music teachers had seated herself at a grand piano in the corner, and was playing the old "Camptown Ladies" while a raucous group of five sang. Valerie recognized a couple of teachers in the group who had lived in the Newark and Irvington areas when they were young—the original "Camptown" during the Civil war—and smiled. The upbeat tempo and jolly voices dispelled any melancholy Valerie might feel when she thought about Stuart.

She was jostled by several people as she stood talking to Al and Bernie, and two more high school teachers joined them. "How many new teachers do we have in the district?" Valerie asked, sipping her drink.

"Nineteen," Bernie said, "in all the buildings. Two at Green Valley Elementary, three at Washington Elementary, and one at Madison Elementary. Five at the middle school and eight at the high school."

Two more of the high school teachers joined them with murmured greetings.

"That's a good number," Valerie agreed. "Have they all joined the union?"

"Everyone at the middle school has," Al said.

"I have to check with the membership chair," Bernie said. "I believe everyone at the high school and Green Valley Elementary did. I'll ask Sue."

"Hello, everyone." The voice came from right behind

Valerie, so close that she could feel a warm breath on her ear.

She recognized the voice at once, and a delicious thrill careened up her spine.

Douglas Cooper stood behind her.

Chapter Four

It had been easy for Douglas to pick out Valerie among the throng of people at the cocktail party. With her almost black, wavy hair, gorgeous face and petite stature, she stood out from the other one hundred plus people jammed into the restaurant. As he drew near her, he could hear her musical voice.

He had wanted to see her again—no, more than that, he was anxious to see her again. The "happy hour" party provided the perfect opportunity. Now he moved forward, greeting her and the group she was with.

She turned to regard him, a startled look on her face.

He couldn't tell if she was surprised, pleased or simply startled.

She was dressed in a bright red sweater and slim black skirt. She wore simple gold hoop earrings that peeked through her shiny hair, and her shoes must have had small heels, because he felt like he was looming over her.

"Hello," she said, her voice breathy.

Bernie greeted him jovially, like he'd known Douglas for years. Al was somewhat more reserved. Bernie introduced him to two English teachers from the high school.

"I'm surprised to see you," Valerie murmured.

"I understand administrators sometimes attend these functions," Douglas said. He'd already spotted the middle school principal in a corner with a large group that was laughing loudly, so he felt perfectly at ease in his statement.

"True," said Bernie, nodding vigorously.

One of the English teachers, a woman in her mid-thirties, was eyeing him suspiciously, but the others all seemed friendly.

"Let me buy you all a round of drinks," he offered. "What can I get you?"

That seemed to relax everyone. They gave their orders, and Valerie, after some hesitation, said, "Just a diet cola, thanks."

He made his way to the bar, stood on line and ordered the drinks. The bartender promised he'd send a waitress over with them and Douglas paid. Returning to the group, he started to ask Valerie a question: "How's that girl in your class, the one who was called—"

"Douglas Cooper!" The loud voice of Jake, the middle school principal, boomed to his right. "How are you?"

Douglas shook hands with Jake, who appeared to be in high spirits. "Great to see you again!" Jake effused. Douglas suspected Jake had had a little too much to drink.

The waitress brought over their drinks, and Jake ordered a round for the people behind him. "I've been meaning to ask you, how's your father and uncle? Tell me what they're doing."

Douglas spent a few minutes talking to Jake. He had the impression that Jake was trying to flatter him for an unknown reason. But then, Jake was the type to fawn over people.

He extricated himself from the conversation, promising to send Jake's regards to his father and Uncle John. Turning back to Valerie and the others, he found them debating the merits of some of the movies that were blockbuster hits over the summer.

Bernie moved on to talk to some other teachers, and soon the two English teachers drifted away. Al had joined a group at a nearby table, which left him alone with Valerie McFadden. "Did you see any good movies this summer?' he asked conversationally.

She sipped her soda. "I only went to the movies twice. But yes, they were enjoyable. How about you?"

"I took my niece and nephew to a couple of kids' movies," he told her.

"It must be difficult raising two children all of a sudden," she said, her voice dropping.

He leaned closer. There was so much noise in the bar area it was getting harder to hear. The singers by the piano were belting out another song, and people at the closest table were laughing hysterically at something.

"Yes, but I love them," he said. Her wide eyes were fastened on him as he continued, "I was really the best one to take them. Their mother's relatives in California hardly know them. My parents and aunt and uncle are getting too old to raise another family. My cousin Sean is a bit on the young side to become a parent—and his sister's still in college. And he just got married. Besides, the kids have always been close with me, so I think they feel more comfortable with me than with anyone else."

"I'm sure they do," she said. "I admire you for raising them."

He was surprised. "You do what you have to. I wouldn't want them to be with anyone else—except their parents, of course." He couldn't help sighing. "They still miss them. I do too."

She nodded. "I understand."

"Do you have brothers or sisters?" he asked.

"A brother and a sister. They're twins," she added. "Jillian and Jared."

"Twins? Are there a lot of twins in your family?"

"A few on my mother's side," she said. "They're twenty-four—four years younger than me. Jillian's finishing law school. Jared's in the navy. He may end up being career military."

"Where's he stationed?" Douglas asked as someone jostled him in passing. The room was growing more crowded by the minute.

"Florida, right now. But it looks like he'll be home at Thanksgiving—which he wasn't able to do last year, so we're happy about that." She took a sip of her cola, eyeing him. "You didn't have to buy drinks for everyone," she said.

"No problem." He shrugged.

"People around here are pretty suspicious of board members," she said abruptly.

He raised his eyebrows. "Bernie doesn't seem to be."

"Well, he's been teaching for a long time. He doesn't get fazed by much."

"So you think people are suspicious because I bought a round of drinks?" he asked lightly.

She flushed, and he had an impulse to reach out and stroke her pink cheek. Even in the dim light, her blush was apparent.

"They might think you were patronizing them."

He shook his head. "I didn't mean it that way—it was just a friendly gesture. Besides," he added, "I thought you teachers were always saying you don't have enough money?"

Now her cheeks grew even rosier. "We don't."

Sensing she was angry—or maybe embarrassed—he made the quick decision to back off. "It doesn't matter," he said quickly. "I just thought it was a nice gesture to start off the school year."

"Oh." She sipped her soda again, looking down for a moment. Then, raising her eyes to meet his again, she added, "I believe you." It came out breathlessly.

She wanted to believe him, Valerie thought, she really did. That Douglas had merely meant it as a friendly overture to the teachers—not in any way as a patronizing gesture. Seeing him at the party so unexpectedly had made Valerie feel off-balance and uncertain. She assured herself her reaction was simple surprise.

But she couldn't help the rush of pleasure she felt when he'd joined her group. And now, standing here conversing alone with Douglas, was, well . . . it was, somehow, intimate. Despite the fact that they were in a crowded, noisy room, she felt as if she and Douglas were somehow closeted together, set apart.

"I see now why you said you were busy the other day," he said, leaning closer. She felt small next to him, even in her heels. "But maybe we can have dinner another time?"

Mixed emotions poured through her. She *wanted* to go. But would it be a good idea?

"I—don't know," she responded truthfully. How could this man take her world and set it spinning every time she was near him? She felt frightened yet exhilarated.

Maybe some time alone would help stabilize her feelings, she thought.

Or maybe it would confuse her more.

Before she could speak, someone pushed her from behind, and she bumped against Douglas. His hand shot out to steady her.

She had to tilt her head to look up into his face. And the look he gave her made her sizzle down to her toes.

She was not the only one who felt this attraction. She was positive that Douglas, too, was feeling something. His eyes widened as they stared at each other.

Valerie stepped back, wanting to put some distance between herself and Douglas, fighting the overwhelming attraction she was feeling.

"Why not?" he was saying as she moved. "Just a friendly dinner."

She was tempted. Dinner alone with Douglas . . . she shouldn't, she thought. Her feelings were strong, and confused. And the fact that he was a board member . . . It would be like walking along the edge of a cliff, she feared.

"I don't think it would be a good idea," she began, when she heard Anne call "Valerie" from behind.

She swiveled to see Anne coming toward her.

"Valerie, I have to get going," she said, and Valerie could hear the distinct note of regret in Anne's voice. "I have to pick up Dylan from my neighbor's." Anne bent closer and whispered, "Guess what? I'm going out tomorrow night with Tony!"

"Good for you!" Valerie said. "You should get out more. Want me to watch Dylan?"

Anne shook her head. "No, tomorrow night he's sleeping over at my parents' house. So it will work out fine."

Valerie was glad. It had been tough for her friend to make time to go out, or even to meet guys. Anne's husband had left her and run off with his secretary years ago, and Valerie knew life was far from easy for Anne. It was time she got out and had some fun.

And isn't the same true for you? A little voice in her mind asked Valerie.

Valerie smiled as she waved goodbye to her friend.

"You look happy," Douglas commented as she turned back to him.

"I am. Anne's going out, and she doesn't get out enough. She's a single mom, and she's struggling to make ends meet. Not to mention the struggle of being a single parent."

"I know how that is," Douglas said, shifting his position.

That made her pause. "Yes, I guess you do. But it's really hard for her. Her ex is constantly late with child support, and on our salaries, bringing up a child isn't easy."

"Is that a plug for a raise?" Douglas asked dryly.

"I—I didn't mean it that way," Valerie said hastily. "But, yes, I believe we need a raise. Especially people like Anne."

"So what about dinner?" he asked, abruptly bringing back the topic.

"I just don't think it's a good idea," she repeated. "I—"

"Hello, Douglas Cooper!" It was Valerie's own school principal, Mr. Hunt. He clapped Douglas on the shoulder. "How's your dad doing these days? And your uncle?"

"Enjoying retirement," Douglas said, turning to speak with Mr. Hunt.

The place seemed to be crawling with administrators,

Valerie thought. She couldn't ever remember seeing so many at a happy hour party—and never a board member. As Mr. Hunt regaled Douglas with tales about bringing his first car to Family Tire for new tires, Valerie murmured a hasty, "Excuse me" and slipped away to the ladies' room.

She wanted not only to freshen up, she wanted a moment to herself. Away from Douglas. Away from everyone. She couldn't believe the intense reaction she had to him every time they were together. A reaction that was exciting—but scary too.

The powder room was at the far end of the restaurant, down a long, dark hallway, past the smoking section. After freshening up, she looked at herself critically in the mirror. Her color was heightened even without applying more blush.

It must be the one drink she'd had, she told herself.

She picked up her purse and left the ladies' room, turning towards the main part of the restaurant, where party noises echoed down the corridor.

"Valerie."

"Oh!" She gasped, realizing a second later that Douglas stood nearby. "I seem to be running into you in dark corridors a lot," she said, somewhat tartly.

He unfurled his long, lean body from against the wall in a shadowy corner. "This time I followed you on purpose," he said lightly.

"Are you into stalking?" She laughed, wishing her heart wasn't beating so hard.

"No," he replied cheerfully. "I just can't seem to get anytime alone with you unless I follow you." He leaned closer.

Douglas wanted time alone with her. The thought reverberated in her mind. For an instant they stared at each other, Valerie clutching her purse as he bent and brought his face closer. The air seemed electrified, charged with tension. She inhaled sharply, smelling the masculine, almost woodsy scent of Douglas' aftershave. Music sounded faintly in the background, and in the shadowy corner the faintest trace of smoke wafted by. For a moment she thought he might kiss her. Her breath jammed in her throat.

"Valerie . . ." he whispered. It was almost an entreaty.

Laughter erupted from down the hall.

They both froze. Then Valerie stepped back.

"That must have been a great joke," she said, waving her hand towards the sound.

"Yeah," Douglas agreed, sounding as if he'd just woken up. "Valerie . . . there's something going on here. I'd like to see you again."

"Going on? Between us?" She couldn't help it; her voice came out as a whisper.

"Yes. Have dinner with me."

She wanted to, but she was still torn—would it be a good idea or a bad one?

"Think about it. I'll call you," he said in a low voice.

"Okay. Maybe." She hated that she sounded so wishy-washy, but she was still unsure.

"I'll call you," he repeated.

"Bye." She said it hastily, then hurried down the hall.

She found a group of teachers from her school and quickly joined them at their table, listening to some funny stories and trying hard not to dwell on thoughts of Douglas.

Douglas stared after Valerie.

He couldn't remember ever having as strong a reaction to a woman as he seemed to be having to Miss Valerie McFadden.

He'd met—and dated—good-looking women before. So it wasn't just her looks. In fact, Hillary had been an extremely attractive woman.

Hillary. He grimaced. His old girlfriend, almost fiancée. Thoughts of her were unpleasant. She was an accountant who was consumed by money. She was always thinking about it. How much did this cost, how much did that person spend, how she could save here and there—so she could splurge on herself.

And how nice it was that Douglas made a good living.

It had taken him quite a few months to realize Hillary was particularly attracted to the fact that he earned a good income. Fortunately he'd also realized his feelings for Hillary weren't lasting. And he certainly didn't intend to spend his life with her.

That had been five years ago, when he was twenty-six. Since then he'd dated casually—at least until he'd taken the children in. He hadn't dated anyone since then.

He wondered if Valerie, being on the negotiating team, was as concerned with money as Hillary had been. She'd made that remark about teachers' salaries. Well, he decided, there was only one way to find out for sure.

He turned to go back to the party, thinking he'd better leave soon. The children were staying with Jessica for a few hours, but he knew Lindsay had a birthday party to go to this evening, and thought he'd spend some one-on-one time with Matthew while she was gone. He started down the hall, when a voice stopped him.

"Hello, Douglas." Kurt Brill stepped towards him.

Kurt was a teacher who had grown up in town, and was a couple of years younger than Douglas. Douglas had known him slightly in high school and now ran into him occasionally.

"Enjoying the party?" Kurt inquired with a sardonic lift of his eyebrows.

By six o'clock people were leaving. A group from the high school decided to eat dinner at the restaurant and invited Valerie to join them, but she declined. She found that the long week, with negotiations, beginning of the year work, and the encounters with Douglas had all combined to tire her out. She was weary and wanted to get home.

Once home, she fed her cats, Cleo and King, then

changed to a comfortable sweatsuit and spent some time playing with them. Her animals never failed to ease her mind.

Valerie's family had always had a dog and cat when she was growing up. She would have liked to do the same, but her small apartment in the three family house and teaching long hours meant a dog would be difficult to care for. And one cat would be lonely. So she'd gone to her local animal shelter two years ago and adopted a young brother and sister. The cats were lovely, white and orange, and fairly affectionate, although Cleo was more fussy than King and sometimes got into a haughty mood.

After rolling some yarn around with them, Valerie settled down with a new novel when Cleo wandered off to stare out the living room window and King disappeared into a corner to sleep.

An hour later, she found herself growing restless and put the book away to go on the computer. She listened to music while she answered some email. When she paused, her eyes went to the pictures of her family and friends on the shelf by the computer. She took down the one of her father when he was around thirty, taken when she was a little girl of two. He was not a tall man, but a handsome one, and his sunny disposition was evident in his smile.

But that had ended with his early death. Her father had only been fifty-four when he died two years before. Remembering how hard he had worked all his life, all the extra jobs he'd taken on, like baseball coach and camp counselor to help support his family, the stress he'd been under, and his sudden and unexpected heart attack, Valerie's throat constricted painfully. Her father was gone, and it hurt. Badly.

If he was here, what would he say? Don't go out with Douglas? Johnny McFadden had never cared for Stuart. Or would her dad recommend that she go for it? So what if he's a board member? Johnny had often talked about how he'd fallen for her mother, Louise, as soon as they'd met at a party. "Sometimes you know it's love right away," he used to say.

Love? More like simple physical chemistry, Valerie told herself.

She sighed and placed the picture back. Maybe she'd turn on the TV and decompress for a while, then turn in early. But thoughts of Douglas continued to haunt her. And they haunted her sleep that night.

Chapter Five

Valerie parked her car and got out slowly, wondering if she was making a mistake shopping here at Family Tire. Two days ago they'd had a torrential rain, and she'd realized she needed new windshield wipers. She could go to the next town to buy them from the discount store, or she could just run over and buy them at Family Tire. She knew from her visits there that they carried standard car accessories and some simple parts. And Family Tire was just on the other side of town, less than fifteen minutes away.

It had been two weeks and a day since she'd seen Douglas—not that she was keeping track, she reminded herself. Two weeks ago she had gone home to visit her Mom for the weekend. Then last Saturday she had spent part of the weekend with her close friend Karen, who lived down the shore. Both weeks at school had kept her busy, and they'd had another meeting of the negotiations team to do some brainstorming. But they'd come up with nothing new to subtract from their list of demands, except, at Bernie's urging, they'd reduced the 20% raise they were asking for over two years to 19%. Even she knew that was inflated and highly unlikely.

During those two weeks, she'd been unable to banish Douglas from her mind. Thoughts of him floated through with annoying regularity. In fact, this past Wednesday night, when she was out with the team, Douglas had called. He had sounded sincere, and asked again if she'd like to get together. But he hadn't left a phone number, and she

was reluctant to call him at work. And she was still un-
decided about the wisdom of seeing him socially.

So she hadn't done anything. But Thursday's rainfall had
proven she needed new wipers, and she'd arrived here to
buy them. Maybe she'd get a chance to see Douglas and
at least thank him for the invitation to get together.

The place looked busy. The temperature was in the low
70s and every bay door of the garage was open. They could
hold ten cars at once. There were a couple of small trucks
there, and around to the side, where the commercial trucks
parked, Valerie spotted two. Family Tires' location just off
Route 80 in Warren County must mean they got a lot of
interstate truck traffic, she concluded, even on a Saturday.

She pushed open the glass doors and entered the crowded
waiting room. People sat in chairs, reading newspapers or
books, some of them talking on cell phones. A harried-
looking mother held a fussy baby. A toddler ran by holding
a balloon, while his father scampered after him. Two older
teenaged boys sprawled in chairs close together, with ear-
phones on their ears and CD players on their laps.

Despite the Saturday afternoon crowd, the place was
well-lit and tidy. Two coffeemakers, a few magazines and
the day's newspaper were scattered on a table on the side,
with a discreet sign that said, "Free Coffee and Tea."

Over the loudspeaker a man was saying, "Mr. O'Hare,
your car is ready." She recognized Sean's voice.

She moved to stand behind the older man as he paid at
the cash register. When he finished, she stepped forward.

"Hello, Valerie," Sean greeted her. So they were on a
first name basis now. "Douglas is in his office but he'll be
back out in a moment."

He thought she was here to see Douglas! Hastily, Valerie
said, "I need new windshield wipers, Sean. How are you
and your wife?"

"Oh, fine." He smiled. "We have plenty of wipers." He
indicated the car parts displayed on the far wall. "You have
anything special in mind?"

She hadn't known there was such variety in windshield wipers. "Just the standard ones," she said.

"Okay—"

"Valerie? Hello!" She turned to see Douglas striding towards her from the office area.

Was she mistaken or did he look delighted to see her? She found herself answering his smile with her own. "Hi," she said.

He was wearing a red and black buffalo plaid flannel shirt and black jeans. In his casual clothes, his muscular body was evident. He looked like he belonged outdoors. And growing up here in the country, he probably spent a fair amount of time outdoors, she guessed.

"It's nice to see you again," he said. Moving closer, his voice dropped. "Did you get my message?"

"Yes, but—you didn't leave your phone number, and I don't have caller ID on my phone."

He shook his head, grinning. "I guess I just forgot. But I'm glad to see you."

"I came in to get windshield wipers," she explained. She didn't want him to think it was entirely because she wanted to see him.

He smiled and proceeded to lead her over to the display to help her select a pair of wipers.

As he helped her, she was once again acutely conscious of his masculine presence beside her and the slight hint of his woodsy aftershave. Here they were, she mused, in a busy tire center, among a number of ordinary people, surrounded by auto equipment. Not exactly a romantic location. And yet it seemed to her that the air sparkled and snapped with electricity.

"Thanks," she said, her voice coming out breathlessly. "This was a big help."

She turned to the cash register.

For a moment Douglas hesitated. "It's yours," he said in a low-pitched voice.

Valerie shook her head; she didn't want a hand-out. "No, don't be silly."

"Well, if you insist on paying . . ." He went up to Sean, who was by the register. "Give Valerie twenty percent off," he said, too low for anyone else to hear.

"Thank you," she repeated as Sean rang up the sale.

Once she had her bag in hand, she gave Douglas a smile and prepared to leave.

"C'mon, I'll put them on the car for you," he offered.

Valerie didn't hesitate. She didn't know too much about cars, and now her brother wasn't around to help her. Even her sister knew more about cars than she did. "That would be a help," she admitted.

They walked out into the cool wind and Valerie indicated her car. It took Douglas less than a minute to put on her new wipers. As she watched, Valerie felt a curious yearning.

Douglas Cooper seemed so nice. Like the kind of guy she would be looking for. If she was actively looking. It was too bad he was on the Board of Ed. Because, even though her experience with Stuart had made her wary, she did want to settle down someday.

"I'll dispose of these," he said, lifting the old wipers.

"Thanks." She took her keys out.

"Wait—do you have a moment?"

She hesitated, then answered, "yes."

"Come on into my office," he invited.

She followed him in back of the long counter and through a doorway that led to a hall. Off the hall were several doors, and Douglas indicated the first one on the right.

His office was small but cozy. The large desk held a new-looking flat-screened computer and a jumble of papers, folders and envelopes. She sat in the chair next to the desk, and studied several photos placed there. There were pictures of a girl and a boy—Douglas' niece and nephew, she guessed. And some family photos, and one of Douglas looking a little younger with a bunch of other friends—probably college buddies. Another one of Douglas with his cousin Sean and another guy who looked very much like both of them.

"Is that your brother?" she asked gently.

He nodded. "That's Keith. People thought he and Sean and I were all brothers—but then, our dads look a lot alike." There was a sad note in his voice.

"You must miss him," Valerie said.

"Yes." He sighed, and studied her. He'd been surprised—and pleased—when Valerie had shown up at Family Tire just a few minutes ago. She looked beautiful, even in the casual pale green sweater and blue jeans she wore. After he had left the message for her a few days ago and hadn't heard back, he'd tried to push her to the corner of his mind. With great difficulty. He kept telling himself it was better if he didn't get tangled up with someone like Hillary—or even someone like Miss Pratt, the teacher who had disappointed him so much years ago.

He hadn't thought about Miss Pratt for a long time, although when he joined the Board of Ed he'd wondered if there were others like her around. Now her name and image slipped back into his mind.

He tensed. Had he been crazy to call Valerie this week? And to invite her into his office now? And yet he wanted to see her. To spend time with her. It was as simple as that.

And he had the strongest urge to see if he was right, or wrong, about the kind of person she was.

She was gazing at him now with sympathy as they spoke about Keith. She, too, had lost a close family member fairly recently. He felt something inside him soften. "How would you like a tour of Family Tire?" he asked suddenly.

Her eyes widened. "I'd like that. But am I taking you away from your work?"

He shook his head. "Saturday mornings are really busy, but after one, things start to slow down." He glanced at his watch. "It's almost two. Things should be getting calmer.

We close at five on Saturdays." He stood up. "Normally, Sean and I don't both work on Saturdays—we take turns so we can have weekends off—but Tim, our next-in-command, had a wedding in Pennsylvania to go to today."

He led Valerie around the center, showing her the huge garage where tires were rapidly changed, the even larger area in the back where they did trucks, and the offices. There was even a small lunch room for the staff, and in one corner, an old computer, small TV, paper and crayons, and Playdough.

"My father and uncle always kept some things here for us when we were kids," he said. "After Matthew, and Lindsay came to live with me, I did the same."

"That's very good," Valerie affirmed. "Then they'll feel at home, and you can keep an eye on them if you have to do some work—and they'll have things to keep them occupied too."

As they walked around, she seemed quite enthusiastic about his place of business, and asked questions about his father and uncle. Douglas felt tempted to put his hand on her shoulder or make some other small gesture. Instead of touching her, he shoved his hands in his pockets.

"I've been here since I was twenty-five—for over five years," he said. "When I finished grad school, I worked in a large corporation for a while, but I didn't like it. Sean's been here a year, since he graduated."

"And before that, your father and uncle ran the business?" she asked.

"Yes. My grandfather, Nathaniel Cooper, actually started it. Now Sean and I are carrying on the tradition." He couldn't help the pride that crept into his voice.

"And your brother, he wasn't interested?" she asked.

Douglas shook his head. "No, Keith was interested in science. He was an engineer. But he did live nearby—only about fifteen minutes from here—so we all saw him often."

"And Sean's sister?"

"Laura? She's in college."

They moved back down the hall. "Since I took over, I've expanded in some areas, like adding quick oil changes to our services, and carrying some auto parts like your wipers." They returned to his office. "What do you think?" he asked lightly.

"I'm impressed," she said, smiling up into his face.

He was unusually pleased by her praise. It was like the sun coming out after a lot of gray days. "Thanks," he said.

She glanced at her watch. "I have one more errand to do. I've got to drop off some stuff I'm donating to the local animal shelter. Their garage sale is next week."

"Do you have animals?" he asked.

"Two cats: a brother and sister." She smiled again. "They keep me company and give me a lot of affection. I would have liked a dog, too, but since I live in a small apartment it's not a good idea. How about you?"

"I have a dog, Riley. She's a mix," he said. "I bring her into the Family Tire several days a week. She's home with Matthew and Lindsay and a babysitter right now." Seeing the interest on her face, he continued. "I got her at the local shelter too. I forgot about the garage sale. I'll have to look around for stuff to donate. We always give a gift certificate to their annual tricky-tray."

"That's great," she said. "Maybe I'll win it next year."

They were silent for a moment.

"So, what about dinner?" he asked abruptly.

She appeared a little hesitant. "Tonight?" But he had the strangest feeling that she wanted to say yes.

"I made plans when I didn't hear from you." Was that a flash of disappointment on her face? "With my friend Chris," he felt compelled to add. "He's a college friend who lives over in Hackettstown."

He saw her relax just the tiniest bit.

For a moment, he regretted making the plans. When he'd decided he needed to get out more, he knew he needed not only to date, but to get together with some of his friends, too. "But how about getting together another time?" he suggested, watching her carefully. "You can join me and the kids next Saturday. We're planning to go pumpkin-picking."

"Okay," she said suddenly. "If we can go in the afternoon—I'm helping at the garage sale in the morning."

More than pleased, Douglas grinned at her. "Great. I'll call you on Wednesday to firm up the time."

"Okay," she echoed.

"And by the way, I asked Matthew and Lindsay if they knew you."

Valerie raised her eyebrows. "You did?"

"Yeah, and they told me Matthew's best friend was in your class last year—Ryan Brady—and that all the students like you."

"I'm flattered," she said. "Ryan is a good student and a really nice kid. I've probably seen your niece and nephew around the school," she added. "Well, I better get going."

"I'll call you," he said, bending towards her. He had a strong urge to give her a quick kiss, and resisted. He'd finally gotten her to agree to going out—even if it was more of a friendly get-together than a date. He didn't want to push Valerie too hard.

"I'll speak to you soon." With a quick smile, she departed.

He watched as she walked down the hall. Even from the back she was attractive. Pretty and cute, he thought. One of these days, he was going to give her that kiss.

He could see why students would like her. She seemed warm and friendly, and she was beautiful. Kids liked that combination.

But he knew from experience that kids weren't always such good judges of character. Look at himself.

Young Douglas Cooper had idolized Miss Pratt, only to find out what kind of person she really was. And in fact, he hadn't been a very good judge of character when he grew up. If he'd seen Hillary more clearly, he would have realized just how much money meant to her. She spent way too much time thinking about it. There were practically dollar signs in her eyes. Only, in his haze of attraction, he hadn't seen it.

Well, he'd get the chance to find out if he was right, and if Valerie was a genuinely nice person. Or if he was wrong. Still, he found himself whistling as he returned to the main room.

After dropping off the donations for the garage sale, Valerie returned to her apartment. Cleo sat by the window, snoozing in a patch of sunlight. She scratched her lightly. A quick look around revealed that King was curled up on her bed, sleeping too. He yawned when she scratched him and promptly went back to sleep.

She made herself some coffee, and thought about the time she'd spent with Douglas. She couldn't help it. He had been so nice, so helpful, with the wipers, and then giving her the tour . . . she had wanted to spend time with him. And when he'd suggested her joining his niece and nephew on their pumpkin-picking trip, it seemed natural to say "yes." It was what she *wanted* to do.

So what if he was a board member?

She stirred milk into her mug. An excursion to pick pumpkins wasn't really a date, was it? It wasn't like they were going out alone or anything. She took her coffee into the small living room. Cleo had moved from the windowsill to the side chair she liked to nap in.

Valerie's answering machine was blinking, and she listened to the message.

It was from Shanna, a teaching friend of hers from Green Valley school who was also single. Valerie had called Shanna and Ruby, another teaching friend, yesterday evening, to suggest they all go to the movies that night. Ruby wasn't able to go because she was going home to Hillside for the weekend. But Shanna had agreed enthusiastically.

But now Shanna's voice sounded congested as she told Valerie she'd woken up with a bad cold, and had decided to stay home.

Valerie sighed. Okay, it wasn't the worst thing in the world to be home alone on a Saturday night. She'd spent many Saturday evenings that way. She wasn't the kind who felt like she had to go out or there was something wrong with her.

Still, she'd felt kind of restless, and had looked forward to seeing a friend. She didn't feel like going to the movies by herself. Most people would be with dates or groups of friends.

Of course, there was always the mall. She enjoyed shopping. But she liked it better when she had money to spend, and she was still being careful. She'd just gotten the bill for the tires.

Well, she had her computer, the TV, and she had stopped at the library before she'd gone to Family Tire. She glanced at the table where she'd put the romance and the mystery she'd checked out. She kicked off her sneakers and curled up on the couch with her coffee, sipping slowly. She was looking forward to seeing Douglas again. Too much.

She really had to get her mind off of him. She reached forward, grabbed the top book, and began to read. But once again she pictured a hero who had a striking resemblance to Douglas Cooper.

Chapter Six

"Goodbye. Have a great weekend!" Valerie said, watching as the last of the students left the room.

"Bye! Bye Miss McFadden!" they called, scurrying down the hall.

The end of the work week: Friday. Satisfaction welled up in her, and she grinned. Today had been a good day.

They'd started this Friday like every other Friday, with the students writing in their journals. A surprising number of them asked her to read their entries, and she'd write back. She had started this project last year, and the students seemed to really enjoy writing without worrying about a grade. A number of them had written about personal problems, sometimes looking for advice or simply reassurance that their feelings were normal.

The students had also had their Friday spelling quiz and the "surprise" math quiz she had hinted at. During their music class, she'd managed to grade both, so she was up-to-date on grading and had her plans for the next week done. She could enjoy the weekend that was about to start.

A weekend with plans she'd been anticipating the entire week.

She went around closing the windows and drawing the blinds. The air was clean with that special crispness of early October. The sun had shone all day, the kids had been well-behaved, and the day had whizzed by.

Valerie loved teaching, but especially on days like this.

Today had been pure delight. She only wished every day in the classroom could be so good.

Earlier in the week she'd had another problem with Scarlett. Over the last few days she'd been forced to watch her carefully, and whenever Scarlett approached Kayla, she interrupted her with things like, "Scarlett, do you need help with something?" or "Scarlett, did you want to tell me something?" to circumvent any name-calling. But Scarlett had said something nasty on the playground several days ago, and Valerie was forced to have a long talk with her. However, she wasn't sure it would do any good, and was considering the fact that she might have to call Scarlett's parents or ask the guidance counselor—who was usually busy—to squeeze in time to speak to Scarlett about her behavior.

But today Scarlett had been fine. Perhaps, she thought hopefully, she would back off and leave Kayla alone.

Valerie erased the board, smelling the pleasant scent of chalk, feeling the dust coat her fingers, hearing as teachers shut doors and began walking down the halls. The teachers were required to stay for a half hour after the students left, except for Fridays.

Friday, she thought for the hundredth time as she straightened her desk.

Tomorrow was Saturday: the day she'd be seeing Douglas Cooper. She had been looking forward to the weekend all week. Looking forward with tremendous eagerness. Not that it was really a date, she repeated to herself. It was more like going out with a group of friends. It just happened that two of them were children.

"Valerie?"

Her thoughts were interrupted as her friend Shanna Goldberg stuck her head in the doorway.

"Oh, hi," Valerie greeted her. "How are you feeling?" Shanna had been out on Monday, but had dragged herself to work Tuesday, still feeling ill.

Shanna was slim, a little taller than Valerie, with pale

blond hair cut short. She'd started teaching second grade here the same year Valerie had, and they'd gotten to be good friends.

"Much better today. I'm glad I'm over that stupid cold." Shanna grinned. "Feel like going to the movies this weekend?"

"I'm really busy with the shelter's garage sale on Saturday," Valerie hedged, deliberately making it sound like it would take all day. She didn't want to share with anyone the fact that she was seeing Douglas. She was uncertain as to how people would react. In fact, she was uncertain as to how she should react.

She had planned to take it easy tonight, turn in early, and get up early in the morning. And by Saturday evening, she guessed she'd be pleasantly tired, between the garage sale and the pumpkin-picking.

"What about Sunday?" she asked.

But Shanna was shaking her head. "I'm going home for the afternoon and dinner. My brother and his wife are visiting for the weekend from Connecticut, and I haven't seen the baby for months." Shanna had grown up in Bergen County, in the eastern part of the state.

"Okay, maybe next week?" Valerie asked.

"Sounds good. Have fun at the garage sale."

"Have a good weekend," Valerie said as Shanna left.

She could hear other people leaving, calling goodbyes. Already one of the janitors was sweeping the hall, his broom making a pleasant whooshing sound.

She finished tidying her desk and picked up her briefcase and light jacket. With one more glance around the room, she turned off the lights and shut the door.

Going to the office to hang up her keys, she found a whole bunch of people leaving at the same time.

"It's going to be a beautiful weekend," Helen O'Bannon was saying. The older woman was always cheerful and one of their best teachers. Valerie liked her a lot.

"That will be good for the animal shelter's garage sale,"

Valerie said. "Thanks for donating those lamps. I'm sure they'll sell right away."

"No problem," Helen said as she hung up her keys.

"Good luck with it," Ruby said as she did the same.

Ruby, another friend, had taught a class for the developmentally disabled in the Jersey City school where Valerie had originally taught. Two years ago Valerie had heard there was an opening for a similar class in Green Valley, and told Ruby about it. She knew that Ruby was gifted in working with special students and had been talking about leaving the city school for quite a while. Ruby had been offered the job, and they'd gotten closer.

"Are you doing anything this weekend?" Valerie asked as they left the weathered brick building and walked down the steps into the fall sunshine.

"Yes. You'll never guess. Last weekend when I was home, my ma told me my old boyfriend James had just called! You know, my boyfriend from college? Seems he just moved back to this area and wanted to look me up. So, we got together for a drink and we're going out on Saturday." Ruby smiled widely.

"Is this the guy you broke up with because you thought you had a crush on his roommate?" Valerie asked.

"That's the one. And I found out later his roommate wasn't half the man he was." Ruby continued to chat as they walked to the parking lot. "But by then James had moved on—literally. He spent several years in Florida. But he missed New Jersey, his friends and family, and he's back now. He's teaching in Newark."

"Well, I hope you have a good time," Valerie said sincerely.

"I have to admit I'm a little bit nervous," Ruby said. "But I'm excited too."

"Go for it!" Valerie said, and they laughed.

Ruby got into her car while Valerie continued to hers. The ride home was usually ten minutes, and today was no different.

Once home, she shed her jacket and pantsuit and got into jeans and a long-sleeved T-shirt. She played with her cats, then made herself a cup of coffee and put her feet up. Now there was nothing to do but relax and look forward to tomorrow.

Douglas pulled up to the three-family house around the corner from Main Street in Green Valley. "I'll be right back," he told Matthew and Lindsay.

Growing up in Green Valley, he knew the streets well, and had recognized which street Valerie lived on when she gave him the address. It was made up of mostly two and three-family homes, built in between the 1920s and 1940s. Now he followed her directions, letting himself into the vestibule and going up one long flight of stairs and then two shorter ones to the third floor. Once at the top landing, he knocked on her door.

"Hi," he heard from behind the door, and then Valerie opened it.

She looked beautiful.

He hadn't expected her to look so wonderful in plain jeans and a T-shirt. Her dark hair was pulled back into a French braid, and her face positively glowed.

"Hi," she said again, breathlessly. He stepped into the room as she said, "I'm ready, I just have to get a sweatshirt."

He glanced around. "How long have you lived here?"

"Since I got my job, four years ago," she answered. "I really don't like those garden apartments that look like everyone else's. And the rents are generally pretty steep. I'm saving," she added, "to someday buy a condo or small house."

"Oh," he said. "I had a condo—still have, in fact. I was living in it and my parents were renting out their house." He shoved his hands in his pockets. They were itching to reach out and touch her cheek. "When Keith died, though,

I decided a house would be better for the kids, and we moved in there, so I rented out my condo."

"That's smart." She nodded her head. "Want a tour of my place? It's small."

He was curious to see the place she lived in, which seemed small but cozy. He'd spotted a worn couch, books, framed photos and CDs lying around. But he decided to wait for the tour. "The kids are in the car. Can I have a rain check?"

"Sure," she replied, and opened the closet to withdraw a sweatshirt. She pulled it on, zipped it partway up, and grabbed her purse. "I'm ready! Bye Cleo! Bye King!"

"Cleo? King?"

"My cats." She grinned. "I talk to them."

Her spirits seemed as high as his, he thought as she closed the door, for which he was glad. He'd had a nagging worry since he first invited her on this little trip that she'd have second thoughts and back out. But he shouldn't have worried. When he'd called her Wednesday, she had sounded like she was looking forward to it.

"What's that say on your sweatshirt?" he asked as she led the way down the stairs. Her gray sweatshirt had red letters, but the hood hid some of them.

She paused and pulled up the hood so he could read.

"If you can read this, thank a teacher," he quoted. "Hmm. Kind of an advertisement for your profession."

"The association made them up and sold them last year." She sounded just a little defensive. "They're nice and warm—and we used the money towards a scholarship for one of the high school students."

"Nice."

She shot him a look, as if she wasn't sure if he was serious or not. He stepped closer as they reached the first landing. He caught a whiff of a light, floral perfume clinging to her. "Who else lives here?" That seemed a safe enough question.

"A divorced man in his forties lives on the second floor.

He travels a lot, so I hardly ever see him. Mr. and Mrs. Burton, the owners of the house, live on the first floor. They're in their sixties and have lived here for years."

They went down the next set of stairs. "It must be hard to bring groceries up."

"I manage," she said with a shrug. "There's just me and the cats, so I don't do much cooking—although I do like to cook."

"How'd the garage sale go?" he asked as they went through the front door.

"Great! I'm glad the weather cooperated. We had a great turn out this morning, and sold a lot of stuff. I'm sure the rest will go this afternoon."

He indicated the red Jeep parked in front of the house. "That's mine."

"Hi!" Valerie said cheerfully to Matthew and Lindsay, who sat in the back, playing with their Gameboy units while they waited.

"Hi, Miss McFadden!" Lindsay said, as Matthew said, "hi" in a quieter voice.

The kids were dressed neatly but casually, Valerie observed, as she put her seatbelt on. Matthew looked a lot like Douglas and his cousin Sean—that strong family resemblance. Lindsay had the same coloring, but her features were different. She must take after her mother, Valerie thought.

"You can call me Valerie," she told them. "Although in school it's probably better if you call me Miss McFadden."

It seemed that her heart had been hammering since Douglas had arrived, and now, sitting in the car with him, she was acutely conscious of his masculine presence. He looked handsome and rugged today, wearing a blue plaid flannel shirt and jeans. His dark hair was a little windblown, and she could smell the same wood-scented aftershave he'd used before. It was strong, as if he'd recently splashed it on.

The garage sale had been fun but she had worked hard,

and at noon she'd hurried home for a quick shower and a
bite to eat before he picked her up. The whole time, she'd
found herself in a state of anticipation. And now that she
was sitting beside him, her emotions had intensified, not
diminished. She tried to distract herself from the heightened
awareness she felt whenever she was near Douglas.

"What are you going to be for Halloween?" she asked
the children.

"A princess!" Lindsay declared.

"A vampire," Matt told her. "What are you going to be?"

"I'm not sure yet," Valerie said. "Last year I was a witch.
This year I want to be something different. But those are
both great ideas! I remember my brother was a vampire for
four years in a row when he was your age," she told Matt.

"Cool," he said.

Douglas had stopped at a red light. "You dress up?" he
asked, and she heard the astonishment in his voice.

"Most of the teachers do," she said. "It makes it more
fun for the students. And we enjoy it!"

"All the *cool* teachers dress up," Lindsay said in a wise
voice.

"Maybe you should too, Uncle Douglas," Matt added.

"I'll consider it," Douglas said with a chuckle.

They talked about school, and the kids' favorite TV
shows, and how they planned to decorate their pumpkins.
They arrived at the farm fifteen minutes later. There was a
big sign saying "Olson's Farm" and another which said
"Pumpkin Picking and Hayrides!" On top of the main
building was the biggest inflated pumpkin Valerie had ever
seen, smiling down on everyone. A policeman was direct-
ing traffic into the field that was being used as a parking
lot. Valerie was amazed to see how crowded it was. They
parked and walked the short distance to the farm. "I've
never been pumpkin-picking before," she admitted as they
walked.

"Then you're in for a treat," Douglas said with a smile.

The sun was shining and it was warmer than she'd expected. She shrugged out of her sweatshirt, tying it around her waist. She was glad she'd worn sneakers because the ground was rough.

Lindsay and Matt led the way to a line that had formed by the barn. "The hayride's over here!" Lindsay said.

"Hayride?" Valerie asked.

"Uh-huh. They take you on a hayride to the pumpkin fields over there." Matthew pointed.

Valerie looked to the right, down a rough road. Acres and acres of fields stretched out, bright with the colors of orange and yellow pumpkins and green vines.

Douglas slanted her a look. "You've never been on a hayride either?"

"No," she said. "Should I worry?"

His blue eyes glinted with humor. "No. Unless we get a driver with aspirations for the Nascar races."

"It's too far to walk when you're holding the pumpkins," Lindsay said.

"It's what we do out here in the country," Douglas added.

"Well, it should be an experience," Valerie said lightly. It could be fun, she thought, although the rutted path winding down to the field looked very bumpy.

"That's the spirit," Douglas said.

A woman was coming down the line, passing out cups. "Try our cider," she was saying. "It's made right here at Olson's."

Valerie sipped the cider. It was sweet, just a little tart, and delicious.

A large truck with side gates pulled up to the front of the line. It was filled with hay on the floor and held upside-down boxes on the sides that served as benches. When the truck stopped, the passengers, holding pumpkins of all shapes and sizes, stepped down.

Their line moved forward. Matt scampered up the steps that the driver had placed by the truck, followed by Lindsay. Valerie walked up the steps and into the truck, which smelled fresh, like hay and grass and sunshine. She took a seat next to the children, and Douglas followed, sitting beside her.

Within a few moments, the truck filled with families, teenagers, men and women with their arms entwined, several older couples, and even a few Asian tourists, exclaiming and talking rapidly as they took pictures. Many of the other people had cameras and video recorders too. Douglas brought out a digital camera and took a picture of his niece and nephew, who grinned up into the camera.

The sunshine, the fresh smells, the joviality of the crowd were all energizing. Valerie smiled up at Douglas, who grinned back. "You'll enjoy this," he said in a low voice.

The truck started and lurched forward. Valerie's hand went out and she hung onto the side. The children were talking and pointing to some turkeys walking leisurely nearby. The truck went over a large bump and everyone leaned to the right. Valerie tried not to shove Lindsay.

"See? It's not so bad," Douglas said.

They worked their way over the rough trail, closer to the fields. The next large bump jolted Valerie smack against Douglas, and she gripped the side of the truck tighter.

He slid his arm around her, offering support. Valerie had an impulse to lean right into his arm, and fought it. He's just helping me balance, she thought.

The road twisted and turned, going downwards, and the truck shimmied as it went over myriad ruts. The hay helped to absorb the shock of the bumps but everyone still swayed and bounced. Valerie constantly slid into Douglas' arm, then away in the opposite direction, as the truck rocked. He swayed along with the truck, absorbing its rhythm, and Valerie tried to match her movements to his to keep her balance.

A minute later they went over a particularly jarring bump. People exclaimed and laughed as they slid off their seats. Douglas's hand moved around Valerie's waist, bringing her closer. Where their legs touched, Valerie felt warmth, even through her denim jeans. She was acutely aware of Douglas' hand casually surrounding her waist. She tilted her head to look at his face, and he turned and met her eyes. He smiled and something inside of Valerie melted like the wax of Halloween candles.

Douglas reached out with his other hand and brushed a wisp of hair out of her face. The gesture was warm and somehow intimate, and a shiver of pleasure wove through her.

The truck stopped abruptly, sending people sliding into each other again. This time Douglas slid toward Valerie, and she braced herself.

"We're here!" a boy nearby called.

The children sprang up, and Douglas stood, drawing Valerie with him.

"That wasn't so bad, was it?" He said it in a teasing voice, but his eyes remained focused on her.

"No," she replied. No, not bad, she thought. In fact, sitting close to him felt wonderful.

They stepped down from the truck. "Let's find some super pumpkins," he said to Lindsay and Matthew.

The kids scrambled ahead, jumping adeptly over vines.

"Here's some!"

"No, too small!"

"Over there!"

Exclamations from them and many other children filled the air. One of the tourists was already snapping pictures. Dry vines crunched under her feet as Valerie cautiously picked her way along, following the children.

She had never seen such a profusion of pumpkins in her whole life. It was a far cry from the farmer's stands she had stopped at once or twice. Acres of color stretched out all around. There were chunky round pumpkins, tall ones, bright orange ones, yellowish ones and even some greenish ones. A few were rotted, with the insides spilling out. But most looked perfectly good.

A couple of crows called overhead, and brilliant sun

poured over the field. She could smell fresh air and hay. The air fairly crackled with autumn crispness.

One man passed by, carrying a fat pumpkin with both hands. "Stella, look at this!"

"Don't pick any with soft spots," Douglas reminded his niece and nephew.

Valerie observed Douglas as he wandered around with the children, pointing out some possible choices, and good-naturedly smiling when they scoffed and declared they had to find their own. She could see how affectionate he was toward them, and they obviously cared about him too. Douglas' brother and sister-in-law had made a wise choice when they left him as guardian for their children.

He walked confidently, occasionally pausing to take a picture, and she got the impression that he was happy with himself and happy with life. Except, of course, for the loss of his brother and sister-in-law.

She walked slowly behind them, enjoying the delight on the children's faces as they studied pumpkins and debated on the merits of different ones. She found herself searching for a pumpkin too. A nice orange one for her classroom. And maybe a small one for her kitchen table at home. She remembered seeing those tiny ones used for decorations near the vegetable stand where they'd waited for the hay-ride.

She was studying one when Matt gave out a yell, signaling he'd found The One. Stepping carefully over the vines, Valerie approached him.

Matt held a tall pumpkin in a kind of oval shape. "He's big," he said proudly.

Valerie smiled. "Nice. He must be the tallest one here."

Lindsay was still searching, and Douglas was watching, smiling. As Valerie drew closer, he turned to regard her.

"Have you found one?" he asked.

"Not yet, but I will," she said.

It was warm in the sun, but here in the fields a breeze

blew, keeping the air comfortable. The rolling pastures, the children and adults laughing and talking, and the colorful blend of pumpkins and warm autumn sunshine made it a picture-perfect afternoon. "Fall really is the most beautiful season," she said as she stepped over to Douglas.

"It's my favorite too," he said, his eyes regarding her warmly. It was like being caressed by a soft wind.

He turned, sweeping his hand to indicate the fields of pumpkins, and the hills beyond, where leaves were already turning red and gold and orange. "This part of New Jersey rivals Vermont in the fall."

"Yes," she agreed. "It's spectacular."

"Beautiful," he said, and his voice dropped to a husky, low note. "And you are too."

"Me?" Valerie, surprised, felt her cheeks grow warm.

"Yes." He reached out, and with a finger, traced her chin. "Beautiful. Stay right there." He stepped back, and before she knew what he was doing, he'd snapped a picture. "Now I have a beautiful woman against a beautiful background."

She felt like her entire body was flushing. "Flatterer." She said it lightly, but his words resonated inside her mind.

"No." He shook his head. "Just telling the honest truth."

"I found one!" Lindsay yelled, interrupting their interlude. She was carrying a very round, very orange pumpkin in her arms.

"Now you have to pick one, Valerie," she said. "And you too Uncle Doug."

It was the first time she'd heard anyone call him Doug. Valerie turned to him. "You always use the name Douglas," she said.

"My parents always called me Douglas. It stuck. And everyone called Matthew by his name, but he started calling me Doug when he was little, and I responded with Matt, and so those names stuck."

"Ahh." Valerie turned to Lindsay. "Want to help me find one?"

Lindsay agreed, and Matt urged Douglas to let him help with his search. The children scattered, and Douglas and Valerie followed more sedately.

"Are you having a good time?" Douglas asked, his voice pitched low.

"Yes, I am!" Valerie declared, and was struck by how true her words were. She *was* having a good time. A great time. Picking pumpkins with the children was a lot of fun, more than she'd imagined. In the beautiful meadow, alive with color and light, happy sounds, and the smell of autumn, she was enjoying the day immensely. Before long the children had helped Valerie find a pumpkin she liked, bright orange and round and not too big.

Douglas also opted for one with good color, larger than hers but smaller than Matt's.

They started the trek back to the spot where the truck picked up passengers, holding their pumpkins carefully. Standing in line, Valerie found herself studying Douglas. He looked totally comfortable and at ease with the kids.

And with her, she thought.

She realized with a start that she, too, felt comfortable, and for the last hour she had forgotten his position and concentrated on enjoying herself with the man he was.

She determined to continue doing so, and to stop analyzing him and the fact that he was a board member—at least for the afternoon.

Once in the wagon, Douglas seated himself beside Valerie and draped his arm around her. Without thinking, she leaned into him.

The ride uphill was longer and just as bumpy. Nestled against Douglas, she felt so comfortable that she didn't mind the jarring and sliding.

Soon they were standing on line to have their pumpkins weighed; Douglas also bought some of the farm's apples. He insisted on paying for Valerie's two pumpkins, despite her protests.

As they returned to the car, he asked, "Anybody feel like ice cream?"

"Yes!" the children proclaimed loudly.

"You knew the answer to that one," Valerie said with a chuckle.

They drove several miles to a snack shop that featured ice cream, soft yogurt and baked goods. The children debated with delight over their selections, picking out their flavors and several toppings. Douglas got some for himself, and Valerie chose a slice of home made apple pie and coffee.

Matt and Lindsay spoke about decorating their pumpkins, and even giving them names. Douglas turned to Valerie and winked.

It was late afternoon when they headed back. Pulling into a space by Valerie's home, Douglas got out of the car as she started to thank him.

"I'll walk you up," he said, and turning to the kids, added, "I'll be back in a couple of minutes."

They had their Gameboys out again and said goodbye as they tapped on the controls.

She got out of the car. The afternoon was just beginning to get cool, but had remained gorgeous. Fall—her favorite season.

She had thought she'd feel tired after the full day she'd had so far, but instead she felt invigorated. She wondered vaguely if she should call Shanna and see if she wanted to take in a movie after all.

Douglas grabbed the larger of the pumpkins. "I'll carry this."

"You don't have to," she said.

"No, it's okay," he insisted.

They walked companionably together and when she opened the door to the vestibule, they started up the stairs.

"Thank you for a wonderful afternoon," she said as they climbed. "I had fun."

He regarded her. "I did too, and so did Lindsay and Matt," he said quietly.

"They are really, really nice kids," she added as they passed the first landing and continued up. "You're doing a great job with them."

He smiled and shrugged. "I try."

"If you ever need help with them sometimes," she added, "just let me know."

"I might, and I'll keep that in mind." He was silent until they reached the top landing and her door. "Actually, there's something you can do," he said.

She paused in front of her door, her keys in hand. Her heart had started to beat harder again. "Oh? What's that?"

Douglas had drawn closer, and now he leaned one hand against the door, close to her shoulder. The air hummed with static. She was suddenly acutely aware of his closeness, of his faint aftershave, of his face only inches from hers. "You can do me a favor." His voice had dropped to a husky timbre that sent a shiver along her spine. He bent closer still.

"What?" she whispered, her eyes on his. His lips looked warm and inviting, she thought dazedly. Was he going to kiss her?

"Have dinner with me tonight," he whispered, and bending forward, kissed her. It was a quick kiss, a warm-and-friendly kiss. But it left her reeling. He lifted his head. "How about it?"

Every part of her was electrified. She gazed at him, and was certain she saw in his eyes the same yearning she was feeling right now.

"With—with the children?" she asked.

"Just us." He dipped his head and kissed her again, longer this time.

The dizzying sensation swept through her.

And suddenly her arms were around his neck, and she was kissing him back. And relishing every exciting moment of it. After a couple of moments he lifted his head again: "Is that a yes?"

"Yes," she whispered.

He kissed her again, swiftly, then stepped back. "Is seven thirty okay?"

At her nod, he touched her cheek lightly, and his finger was warm as it stroked down her face.

"I'm looking forward to it already," he said.

Chapter Seven

Douglas knocked lightly on the door to Valerie's apartment.

He could hear faint music, then the click of heels against wood. There was the sound of the knob turning, and she opened the door. She looked stunning.

"Hi!" she greeted him. "You're a little early. Come on in—I'm just about ready."

He stepped in as she closed the door and went back to fastening a hoop earring.

She was wearing an aqua sweater and short denim skirt that revealed perfectly-shaped legs. She had taken her hair out of the braid and it now waved around her shoulders, inviting his fingers to sift through it. She was smiling softly and for a moment, he had the overwhelming desire to kiss her again.

The kiss they'd shared briefly just hours before had been amazing. He wanted to experience that intense pleasure again. And again.

"Just give me two minutes," she said, and dashed into the adjoining room.

He looked around the small living room. The worn brown and beige couch had a few comfortable pillows tossed on it. There was a large beige chair on the side by the window, looking a little newer. A white and orange cat sat on it, staring at him arrogantly. As he regarded it, the cat yawned, deeming him boring, he presumed.

"Hi," he said to the cat. It blinked.

Across from the couch was a medium-sized TV, a VCR and a small CD player on a wall unit. On the shelves were CDs, mostly of popular music and some jazz, he noted as he examined the titles. There were some videos too. And there was a bookcase filled to the brim with books. He checked the authors. They appeared to be mostly romance novels, with a few bestselling mysteries thrown in. A couple of houseplants, candles and photos were scattered around.

"Would you like that tour now?" Valerie asked from the doorway.

"Sure," he said.

"This was originally a two-family house," she began. "But they converted the attic into an apartment forty or so years ago. That's Cleo, over there," she indicated the cat sitting on the chair. She stepped through a door into her bedroom, a room oddly shaped as a T. "You can see the lay-out's a little strange."

The room held a bed with another cat asleep on it, a night table, two small white dressers and a closet. There was another bookcase here as well, chock full of more books. Plenty of photos were positioned on the furniture.

From there they walked into a surprisingly large kitchen.

"This is the largest room in the apartment," she said, sweeping her hand.

The room was painted a sunny yellow. He observed that she had a good amount of cabinets and counter space. A newer kitchen set sat towards the side of the room. One corner of the room had been set up as an office, with a desk, computer, some shelves with books and more photos. In another corner was an opened door that led to a bathroom.

"And there's a back door, although those stairs are pretty steep," she said, pointing to the back. "Like I said, it's a strange layout. But it's a nice, quiet place to live and the rent's very reasonable."

"It's nice and cheery," Douglas said. "Especially the kitchen."

"Yes, it is. I would have liked something a little bigger—but, oh, well. At least here I can save a little money. Someday I'll have a bigger place."

He stopped to look at the photos on the desk. There was Valerie in a cap and gown, surrounded by some young women and men similarly garbed. They were laughing and smiling.

"My graduation from Kean University," she said.

"Your family?" he asked, pointing to a photo of Valerie with a young woman and man who looked remarkably alike, and two adults.

"Yes. That's my sister and brother—Jillian and Jared—did I tell you they're twins? And my parents. This was taken four years ago, at a cousin's wedding."

Valerie bore a striking resemblance to her father, who was a good-looking man. Her brother and sister looked more like her mother, who was also attractive, but they had their dad's dark coloring.

There was also a single black and white photo of her father, displayed prominently. With longer hair that had no visible white in it, and an unlined face, it appeared this picture was taken a long time ago.

"That was a photo of my dad taken for his school's yearbook when he had only been teaching a couple of years," she said, a note of sadness evident in her voice. "I always liked it."

"He was a handsome man," Douglas said. "It looks like he was personable too."

"Oh, he was," she agreed. "Everyone liked him." Once again he heard that sad note in her voice. She turned her face away, and he wondered if her eyes had tears in them.

He shoved his hands in his pockets, looking for an alternate subject. "I see you like to read," he said. "It looks like you read a lot of the same stuff as my sister-in-law, Jessica. Romances and mysteries."

"Yes." She regarded him with a slight smile. "I guess I've loved romances ever since I read fairytales growing up."

"Like the handsome prince coming to the rescue of the beautiful princess?"

"Something like that," she said lightly. "Although today, they would just as likely write that the princess used a karate chop to rescue the prince from the dragon or what-ever."

He laughed. "True."

"I'll just get a jacket and we can go," she said.

They went back through the bedroom—it really was a strange lay-out, he thought—and she paused to scratch the cat under the chin. He looked content, shut his eyes, and promptly went back to sleep. "This is King," she said.

Douglas went over and slowly extended his hand. The cat opened his eyes and stared. He scratched King behind his ears, and the cat purred.

"Nice to meet you, King," he said.

"And," she continued as they entered the living room, "Cleo, is his sister." Cleo blinked as Valerie stroked her too. When Douglas went to scratch her, she got up and jumped to a table.

"It takes her longer to get used to people," Valerie said. "You said you have a dog?"

"Yes," he said. "I was thinking of adopting one, and after I got the kids, I thought it would be good for them. Dogs give you a lot of love," he added. "My family's always had dogs."

She nodded. "I know."

They talked about animals as they went down the stairs and left her home. She asked about the children, and he told her that Sean and Jessica were watching them over at their house, and had brought in pizza. "They are really nice kids," she told him again. "You must be proud of them."

"I am." He opened the car door for her. "And they liked

you a lot too." He didn't add that Lindsay had asked if
Valerie was his girlfriend.

"Just a friend," he had assured his niece. Girlfriend? He
wasn't ready for anything like that. The truth was, he wasn't
sure if he was ever going to get married. Things hadn't
worked with Hillary, and now he had a ready-made family;
he didn't really need a wife.

The ride to the restaurant took about a half hour. He'd
picked an Italian restaurant in western Morris County, a
quiet, simple place with delicious food. As he drove, they
talked about music they liked.

"This is such a beautiful area," Valerie said, switching
the topic. "I love western New Jersey. Where I grew up,
it's so crowded."

"It is a beautiful area," Douglas agreed as he pulled into
the parking lot. "Although it's more built up then when I
was young, the character of Green Valley hasn't changed
that much. It's still an old-fashioned town."

The restaurant was busy but not jammed, and they were
seated after a few minutes. She saw several women turn to
stare at Douglas as they were led to their table. Valerie was
secretly glad that Douglas had chosen something outside of
Green Valley. She didn't relish running into people who
might know them both. She was more than a little uncomfortable with actually dating a board member. And it was
a date. There was no getting around that.

But she'd wanted to go—more than that, she'd been so
eager she had barely considered saying no. Their outing
this afternoon had been fun, and she'd found herself wanting to spend more time with Douglas.

She looked over the menu, and ordered chicken parmi-
ginia with spaghetti, one of her favorite dishes. Douglas
ordered the chicken cacciatore, and garlic bread for them
both.

A waiter came and brought them a hunk of cheese, light-
ing the dark green candle on their table. After they ordered

he brought them wine, and Valerie sipped, studying Douglas. He was devastatingly handsome in his sports jacket and tie. Plus, he exuded a certain air of assurance, of masculinity, that was dangerously appealing. Valerie knew she was not immune to its power.

She placed her wine glass on the table and reached for the small loaf of warm, crusty Italian bread, cutting off a thick slice for herself, and one for Douglas. She handed it to him and their fingers touched, just a slight brush, but it made her fingers tingle. She met his eyes. Did he feel it too?

Wanting to bring things back down to earth, Valerie asked about the house where Douglas and the children lived. He described the old Victorian where he'd grown up, and how he'd recently had some renovations done to make it more modern—updated electrical wiring to keep up with the computers, a finished playroom in the basement he'd worked on with a couple of friends, and fencing in the yard.

She asked him about growing up in Green Valley, and he told her about some of the local lore. She'd heard the tale of the one-handed ghost that haunted the old train tracks in the area from Morris County through Warren County, and he described how he and his friends had driven out to the purported location of the most frequent sightings. And how, during one full moon, they'd all seen an eerie light.

"Just like the lantern he was holding in his hand when he died," Douglas said, his voice definitely sounding spooky.

Valerie couldn't help shivering. "That's quite a story. I read scary stories to my class around Halloween, after they've done their work. I'll have to remember that one. Although they may be a little too young for it."

"Oh, I knew that story from the time I was six," Douglas declared. "And I've told it to Matt and Lindsay. They think it's cool."

"Cool . . . and scary," she said.

"How do you like Green Valley Elementary?" he asked as their garlic bread arrived.

"I like it a lot," she said. "The kids are pretty nice for the most part, and the parents care without being too interfering. Actually, they care a lot more than the parents in the urban district where I used to teach. I love teaching here." She nibbled on the tasty garlic bread.

"What kind of interference do you mean?" he asked, furrowing his brow.

"Well, in some districts where my friends teach, there are parents who come in and try to tell the teachers how to do their jobs. People think that because they went to school, they know about education. But what does a dentist know about teaching reading to a slow learner? I wouldn't tell my dentist how to drill teeth."

Douglas laughed. "They're probably just concerned. Now that I'm kind of a parent, I can understand that."

"It's good to be concerned," Valerie agreed, "just not bossy." She paused, then said in a carefully neutral voice, "How would you feel if a customer tried to tell you how to run your business?"

"Some of them do," he said.

She'd never thought of that. "Oh."

"If a customer had a suggestion," he continued, "I'd listen, and think about what they said. It might be that they had a valid idea that would improve things."

They were treading on difficult waters here, Valerie thought, and tried not to be too controversial. "Like when the parents suggested new marching band uniforms and lobbied the board to spend money on them. They were badly needed, but the board didn't allocate the money until the parents raised their voices."

"Exactly." Douglas reached for a second piece of garlic bread. "A lot of the parents want a back-to-basics approach today, and I agree with that. We should definitely have the arts, of course, but we also need to emphasize reading and math."

Valerie nodded. "I agree." Well, she thought, that was nice!

"For example, we need new math textbooks badly," he continued. He appeared to be studying her for her reaction.

"That's true," she said. Maybe Douglas' views weren't so very far off from the teachers' ideas after all. "But I remember when they purchased a whole new set of social studies books for the elementary schools two years ago. The ones we were using were still good—in many ways, better than the new ones. They wasted money ordering new ones. They would have been better off using the money for something else—like a part-time resource room teacher." She eyed him for his reaction, wondering if she should have withheld the last comment.

"Or maybe for more supplies for the special ed students," Douglas stated.

They stared at each other for a moment. Valerie thought she detected a challenge in Douglas' eyes. She really didn't enjoy verbal sparring, so she decided to meet the challenge head-on. "You really don't think teachers deserve much money, do you?" She asked the question directly, but in the soft, non-threatening voice that she often used in class. "Why?"

Douglas looked taken aback. She guessed he hadn't expected her to be so forthright. He hesitated for a moment, then said, in an equally pleasant voice, "I know that there are some truly dedicated teachers out there. From observing you, I'm positive you're one of them. But there are a lot of teachers who aren't."

"Why do you say that?" Valerie questioned.

"I'll tell you a true story," Douglas said, reaching for his wine glass and taking a drink. "I was in seventh grade. I had a really gorgeous teacher, Miss Pratt, for English. All the boys were crazy about her—well, we were all adolescents, and she was hot-looking." He grinned.

Valerie felt herself tensing up.

"One day, I stayed after school to make up a test I'd missed when I was sick. I was in the room, working, when another teacher stopped in to talk to Miss Pratt. They went out into the hall. I guess they figured I was concentrating on the test and not listening, but they weren't very quiet, and I could hear everything they said.

"Miss Pratt started complaining about the school, and how she couldn't wait til the next vacation. She said she didn't like teaching at all, and that she was just in it for the vacations. And the money, although she didn't consider that great, except that she figured getting almost ten weeks off every summer made up for it." His voice rose with indignation and his expression darkened. "Then she started to laugh. She told the other teacher how ridiculous she thought all us kids were. She knew all the boys had crushes on her but she didn't like us. She couldn't wait for the summer vacation. I felt sick as I listened to her nasty remarks."

Valerie felt sympathy for the young, impressionable teen who had been so disillusioned by the object of his affection. She felt anger, too, toward the teacher he'd admired. She knew a few people like that herself, and hated that they gave her profession a bad name. It made it more difficult for the truly dedicated teachers out there. But she felt miffed at Douglas as well. Surely it was unjust to judge all teachers badly because of this one!

The waiter brought their salads, and after he left, she responded, thinking carefully about her words. "I'm sorry you had such a hurtful experience, especially at such a— tender—age. It must have been very painful for you. And, unfortunately, Doug—" the name slipped off her tongue— "I have met a few teachers like that myself." She thought of one at the middle school, who sometimes called in sick during the nice weather to go golfing. But she certainly wasn't going to bring up Mr. Bellar with Douglas. "I agree," she continued, "that those people should not be in the classroom."

She shifted slightly in her seat. The savory aroma of the garlic bread wafted up to her. "But it's not really fair to judge us all poorly because of a few bad teachers. There are bad examples in every profession—doctors, lawyers, accountants, even—" she gave him a grin—"even tire center owners, I'm sure." She lifted her water goblet, and took a sip of the cold liquid.

"Of course I don't think you're all like that," Douglas said, a hint of impatience in his voice. "But there are a fair number of teachers like Miss Pratt out there. Cold, uncaring, just doing the minimum to get by. Look at Bellar."

Valerie's mouth dropped open, and she shut it quickly. So the board members knew about Bellar's golf outings.

She didn't address that topic. "But look at the others," she challenged, "like Mrs. Dolan, who spends her own money for supplies her class needs—and she treats each student to ice cream on their birthdays—"

"Oh, I know that," Douglas said, his voice more pleasant. "Believe it or not she was my kindergarten teacher. But there is still a lot of dead wood out there. And because of New Jersey's tenure laws, we can't get rid of them."

"We need tenure!" Valerie said hotly, sitting up straight. "Do you know how much politics is involved in a school system? Without tenure protection, many good teachers would lose their jobs—say, if the relative of a board member wanted their job, or if they disagreed on a political issue with the administration—" She stopped abruptly. Douglas was smiling. He was baiting her, she realized, trying to see what kind of reaction he got.

She sent him a silent, accusing look.

He sighed. "Okay, I didn't mean to get you all worked up, I just wanted to see your reaction. I suspected you were a gung-ho union activist."

"Well, yes," Valerie said. "But I like to think I'm a reasonable one."

The waiter brought their main courses, which looked and smelled delicious, and they paused until after he left. Then Douglas began again: "I realize tenure was started to protect teachers," he said, his voice even. "I'm not suggesting we do away with the whole system. But I do get disgusted by teachers who demand pay raises when they don't care about their students and put in the minimum effort on their job."

"There are a lot more teachers who DO care," she said, keeping her voice pleasant too. "Teachers who spend extra time helping students, who try to come up with creative lessons. I could go on and on. Teachers like . . ." she stopped, as her father's face came to mind.

"Like . . . ?" Douglas prompted.

"Like . . . my father," she said, her voice dropping.

"Tell me about him," Douglas said, his tone softening.

"He was—wonderful. I adored him," Valerie said. "He was funny and smart and interested in all kinds of things. And he told great stories. We all—my sister and brother and I—looked up to him. I remember him sitting at the dining room table when I was little, correcting papers and working on his plans for his classes. Or studying for his Master's degree. He always tried to create interesting lessons for his students," she continued. "Every year, he held a Famous Historical Personalities Day, and students would dress up as someone from history. My dad always did too. One year he was Napoleon." She started to laugh, remembering how funny he looked. "Johnny McFadden was a very popular teacher."

"He sounds like he must have been," Douglas said, twirling spaghetti on his fork.

"But as I grew up, he was home less and less often," she said, and heard the wistful note in her voice. "He took on other supplemental jobs. Coaching the school's baseball team, advising the Future Teacher's Club, some tutoring on the side, that sort of thing. It's expensive to bring up three children, and he wanted my mom home when we were small. Once we were all in school my mom went back to work at the bank. But my dad was determined that we would all go to college—even if we commuted, like I did. And he wanted nice things for us, like summer camps and good clothes and carpeting in our rooms. So he worked hard and took on extra jobs to make money." She swallowed. "You see, where he taught the pay wasn't very good, especially when he started, and the raises didn't keep up with inflation.

"Even when we were all older, he kept it up," she continued. "He said he was saving money for our weddings. And my sister was planning to go to law school, and . . ." She paused again. "One afternoon, he was staying late at school for baseball, and he didn't feel so good. Someone suggested he go home, but he insisted he had to stay and finish the practice. Then he was heading out to tutor a student. He—never made it." She fought the tightness in her throat that thoughts of that day always brought on. "On the way to the kid's house, he must have felt something, because he pulled into a parking lot and turned off the car. He must have been reaching for his cell phone, because they found him with his hand in his pocket. He had a heart attack and—died instantly." She choked on the last words.

Douglas put down his fork, and covered her hand with his large, warm one. "I'm so sorry," he said quietly.

Valerie looked down, then up at him. She knew there were tears in her eyes. "If only he hadn't worked so hard. He was a gifted teacher, a true professional, but he didn't make the kind of money other professionals did. So he scrounged up other jobs, worked long hours to take care of us . . ." She pulled her hand away and groped for her purse. Pulling out a tissue, she blew her nose. "He was only fifty-four."

"I *am* sorry," Douglas repeated, his voice ringing with sincerity. "I can see it was tough for you."

She put the tissue away and fought to control the tears. She was struck by the thought that Douglas, too, knew what it was like to lose a loved one—someone even younger than her father.

"I know you're hurting too," she said quietly. "And your brother was much younger than my father."

"Yes, and killed by a drunk driver," Douglas said, his mouth twisting. "But back to your father," he said, "is it possible that he was a workaholic by nature?"

"No," she said, shaking her head vehemently. "That wasn't it. I heard him talk many times to my mother about the low salaries in his school district, and how he needed extra money to support us, even if it wasn't anywhere near a lavish lifestyle. It really troubled him that, with all his education, the hours he put in and devoted to his job, he was paid poorly."

"And yet you went into teaching too," Douglas observed.

She answered his unasked question. "Yes. I guess I caught his enthusiasm for the best aspects of the job, and I loved working with kids, especially the younger ones. I like helping them to understand. Plus," she said, pausing to reflect, "I was young and idealistic. I thought it would be different for me, that I could do something to change the system."

"Ah." Douglas let out a long breath. "So that's it."

"Yes," Valerie agreed. "I told my dad once that it might have been better if he spent his time negotiating with the team instead of taking on other jobs." She could almost taste the bitterness, competing with the flavorful tomato sauce on her chicken. "Unfortunately, although teachers have started getting paid better the last few years, it came to late to make a real difference for my dad."

"That is a shame," Douglas said.

"So I guess you can see why I joined the negotiating team," she finished on a shaky note. She was a little surprised to find she'd confided so much to Douglas. Only a few of her friends from Green Valley knew the whole story.

"Yes, I can see why," he agreed. "At first I thought you might be . . ." He stopped.

"Might be what?" Valerie asked after a moment.

"One of those—you know—money hungry women." He said it slowly.

"Money hungry women?" Valerie felt puzzled. It sounded like he was talking about someone specific. She probed a little. "Like someone you know?"

"Someone I knew," he said, and now his voice held a sardonic note.

"Tell me about her," she said, in a calming voice.

He stopped. Valerie waited, hoping he'd talk. She could see the hesitation in his face.

"Please," she added.

"We were going out for a while," he said suddenly. "I was thinking maybe we'd get married . . . Hillary was a certified public accountant. At first I thought she was just thrifty—like a lot of accountants."

"Yes," she encouraged him. "I know some like that."

"Then, gradually, I realized that money meant a lot to her. More than people, more than anything." His face darkened. "I told her I wasn't like that, and we broke up. Last I heard, she was married to another accountant, living in a fancy house."

"And you thought I was like her?" Valerie asked.

"Yes." His frown disappeared. "But I realize now you're not. You're negotiating because—well, because of your father, and wanting better things for teachers."

"Thank you," she said quietly. But negotiations appeared be a touchy subject, and they were getting along right now. So as not to dwell on anything controversial, she switched the topic slightly. "I was wondering," she said gravely, "why a guy as handsome and friendly as you wasn't married already."

"Oh." For a moment, he looked surprised by her statement. "Well, after Hillary. I seemed to meet other women like her. And then, my brother died. And once I had the children, I didn't have the time. Or the inclination," he added, more darkly.

"Why?" She took another piece of the spicy chicken.

"Well I kind of have two children already. I'm not sure I'll get married. I haven't really given it any thought. I mean, I already have a family," he finished.

Valerie felt the blood drain slowly out of her cheeks. Maybe out of her soul, she thought. He didn't have the inclination to get married?

Douglas Cooper was another Stuart.

She clutched her fork hard. The cold metal bit into her.

Now she really did taste something bitter. Of all the men to be attracted to, the last thing she needed was another one like Stuart. A man who wanted to have fun, but no marriage or family ties. No commitments. She swallowed, and reached for her water goblet, gulping down cold water. Why, oh why, did she have to feel attracted to these guys who didn't want what she wanted? Alright, maybe Douglas was a little different. But if she'd had any thoughts, even the slightest hope, of something more than friendship with him, she'd better quell the idea now. Stomp on it and lock it away.

Build a wall around her heart. A high wall.

"Valerie?" He was looking at her with concern.

Something of her dismay must have shown in her face. She pulled herself together. She was a decent actress. She had learned how to hide her distress from her classes when something bad happened. That's what she'd do now.

"You *do* have a family," she said. "A very nice one, in fact." She bent her head and cut up another piece of chicken.

With the amount of sharing they'd been doing, she'd had a fleeting thought about confiding in Douglas about Stuart. But she wasn't going to dredge that up now.

Instead, she back-tracked to the topic of teachers. "Maybe you should visit the schools again," she said, "and stay longer." She saw fleeting surprise on his face, and knew he hadn't expected the change in subject. "Then you can really observe what's going on. Not all of the people on the negotiating team are like your old girlfriend. Most aren't consumed with thoughts of money—just with trying to make ends meet."

"Maybe I'll do that." He said it slowly, and she thought he looked uncertain. Maybe about the idea, maybe about her swift change of subjects.

She went back to asking him about some of the local legends as they finished their meal. Valerie was full and didn't want a large dessert, so Douglas ordered a cannoli to share.

They continued to speak about the area, but Valerie felt an increasing strain. They had both gotten into emotional experiences and issues, but she sensed their viewpoints were as far apart as ever. They were doubtful, maybe even suspicious of each other, she thought. At least she was. And she suspected she cared about his opinions way too much.

But she managed to keep the conversation light, to laugh at some of his stories, and to tell a few of her own. Although hers weren't as funny—as a kid, Douglas had been more daring than she had.

She kept her distance emotionally, though, feeling almost as if she was watching herself with Douglas, like it was another Valerie McFadden talking to him and not herself.

They left the restaurant and drove back to Valerie's home. Douglas had flipped on the radio to the local oldies station, and a Rolling Stones song was playing in the background. "I noticed you have a wide variety of musical interests," he said.

They discussed some of their favorite rock groups, and although Valerie continued to feel tense, she was proud that she was able to converse casually with Douglas again.

As Douglas searched for a spot to park on her street, Valerie wondered if she should invite him in for a cup of coffee. It wasn't too late, and she hated to have the evening end on a strange note. And yet, how could it not? He was clearly not interested in some of the things she wanted— marriage, family, teachers' raises. Yet despite this, she found herself saying, "Would you like to come in for a couple of minutes?"

"Yes," he answered swiftly.

It's no big deal, she told herself as she fished in her purse for her keys. They climbed the stairs together, and she fit the key into the lock on the door. She'd left a lamp on in the living room. In the low light, she shed her jacket and saw Douglas loosen his tie. Neither one of the cats was in the room.

"Would you like coffee or cocoa or a soda?" she asked. "I don't have any liquor except some white wine."

"Cocoa would be nice," Douglas said, settling on the couch.

Valerie went into the kitchen to make instant cocoa from a mix. When she returned with two mugs, Douglas had his jacket and tie off, and his shirt open at the neck.

He looked handsome and far too attractive, so Valerie's heart tripped and started beating faster. The couch suddenly seemed too small. She sat on the opposite end, and bent her head to inhale the comforting, homey scent of the cocoa. For a moment there was an awkward silence.

Then Douglas said, "Valerie?"

She looked at him.

"I think I have a better handle on how you feel regarding negotiations," he said slowly, as if he was choosing his words with care. "And why you feel the way you do."

She suddenly felt a great rush of relief.

Maybe he did understand. Or was trying to.

But that was no longer the biggest chasm dividing them. Still, she couldn't fight the feeling of gladness creeping through her.

Before she could even think, she found herself responding. "And I understand better how you feel—about teachers who slack off."

He grinned. "Good. Now we can put that behind us." He placed his mug on the side table and leaned closer, plucking hers from her hands and depositing it next to his.

She caught her breath.

He cupped her face. She felt a tremor go through her as he bent his head closer and kissed her. The kiss was gentle, tentative at first. And then his mouth pressed firmer into hers, and without thinking she slid her hands around his warm neck.

Douglas enfolded her in his arms, holding her tightly.

He kissed her lips again and again. Valerie felt as if the world was spinning, as if the whole room was tilting, engulfed in warmth. Blood seemed to rush from her head to her fingers and toes.

"Oh, Valerie . . ." Douglas murmured, breaking the kiss for a moment. His fingers tangled in her hair. A sudden thump nearby startled them, however, and a feline yowl sounded complainingly nearby. "Wh-at?" Douglas sounded dazed as she pulled back.

Cleo stood there, staring at them with an accusing look. Valerie fought a desire to laugh. Things were so intense that perhaps they could use some comic relief, but she didn't want to insult Douglas.

But now he was grinning too.

"Guess she doesn't want me taking all your attention," he said.

"Cleo," Valerie said lightly, "I'm a big girl; you don't have to chaperone."

From the dark doorway to her bedroom, King glided out, and jumped up on the table near Valerie.

"Maybe that's my cue to leave." Douglas spoke slowly, and Valerie could hear reluctance in his voice. He stood up, and she followed him to the door.

"I had a very nice time tonight," she said, her voice low, sounding huskier than usual to her own ears. "And today too. It was a lot of fun."

"So did I," he said. And bent forward to give her another quick, hard kiss on the lips. "A lot of fun." He paused. "I'll call you this week."

"Okay," she whispered, and he smiled and left.

She listened as his footsteps went down the stairs, then shut the door and locked it, before turning to brace herself against it and stare at the cats. Her lips still burned from the intensity of Douglas's kiss. A kiss that affected her from her lips down to her toes.

And there was a surprising, achy feeling in her heart.

She was afraid she was feeling too much for Douglas Cooper—emotions she should beware of.

Chapter Eight

The phone's shrill ring startled Valerie. Placing the teaching journal she was reading beside her mug of cocoa, she leaned over and picked up the phone. "Hello?" she said as rain spattered against the living room window.

"Hi Valerie. It's Douglas."

She tensed up. She had been debating since Saturday night whether or not it was wise to continue to see him. On one hand, he was a board member, which meant he was on the opposing side from the teachers. And, even worse, he'd admitted he wasn't thinking about marriage while she knew she wanted a husband and family.

She had finally called her friend Karen on Sunday night for advice.

"Maybe it's better like this," Karen had said. "You can just have a good time with him, then walk away, knowing it will never amount to anything. You won't have to worry about getting fully attached to a board member.'

Maybe, Valerie had thought, Karen was right. But her thoughts on this rainy Monday had continued to swirl in confusion.

"Oh, hi, Douglas," she said now.

"I, uh, wondered if you could give me a hand with something," he said, sounding uncertain himself. "It has to do with the children."

Just the mention of the children made her soften. "If I can. What is it?" she asked.

"The day after we went pumpkin picking, Lindsay informed me that her mom always made pumpkin cookies with her and Matt. She wants me to do the same. She seemed so sad when she asked me, like it meant a lot to her." He paused, and she could hear the catch in Douglas' voice.

Her heart went out to his nephew and niece. Even with a loving uncle, it must be very difficult for them.

Douglas continued. "I hate to disappoint her, but—I know next to nothing about baking. I was hoping you could help us out."

Eagerness washed over Valerie, and she was pretty sure it wasn't just eagerness to help Matt and Lindsay. "The poor kids," she began. "It's tough for them. I do like to bake, and I'm sure I can find a recipe for pumpkin cookies somewhere. We can even decorate them."

"Oh, that would be great." She could hear the relief in his voice. "I want to try to keep the traditions the kids had with Keith and Denise—I think it will help them deal with things."

"It's a good idea," Valerie concurred. "And a way to remember the good times they spent with their parents. I'll be happy to help." She meant it.

Of course, seeing Douglas would be an added bonus, her mind whispered.

"Thank you!" he declared. "How about Friday, after school? Then we don't have to worry about homework right away, and we don't have soccer practice or dance class. We can order a pizza for dinner too."

"Okay," Valerie agreed. "I'll bring the ingredients. Do you have cookie sheets?"

She went over with Douglas what utensils he needed, and he promised to buy what he didn't have. "And I'll reimburse you for the food ingredients," he said.

"Thank you," she said quietly. "I appreciate that."

They agreed on four o'clock, since Sean was the one who closed the center on Fridays. Douglas asked her how she was doing, and they spoke for a few minutes.

"I better make sure the kids are getting ready to go to sleep," he said. "But I'll see you soon."

"Okay," she said. "Bye."

"Bye."

She hung up the phone slowly, then huddled into a corner of the couch.

Cleo, in her favorite chair, lifted her head to stare at Valerie for a moment before deciding nothing exciting was happening, and buried her face in her fur again.

It was no big deal, Valerie told herself. Just baking with the kids. Of course she would help out.

But, even on this rainy evening, there seemed to be a warm glow in the room.

As usual, the teachers entered the board conference room first. Valerie placed her briefcase on the table in between Phyllis' and Anne's briefcases, and then went to leave the muffins she'd brought on the table with the coffee. She hoped her inner turmoil didn't show.

What was it going to be like, she wondered, seeing Douglas again in his board capacity?

Douglas was in her thoughts more often than she liked over these past few days. At odd moments she'd see his image in her mind, looking rugged like he had when they were pumpkin-picking, or looking handsome and sophisticated like he had when they'd gone out to eat. And, of course, she couldn't help replaying his kisses in her mind. Even thinking about them made a tremor skim up her spine.

What's more, today at school, she'd thought several times about his call the evening before, and about baking with the children on Friday.

"Let's hope the board is more reasonable this time," Phyllis said as Valerie sat down beside the older woman.

"Yes," Valerie murmured.

Anne gave her a quick smile. She was smiling a lot these days. Since her first date with Tony, Anne had met him for

coffee a couple of times after school and had gone out with
him again this past Friday.

Valerie returned her friend's smile, then shifted in her
seat as the board members entered the room.

Douglas was the second one to walk in.

He wore black jeans and a gray sweater over his shirt.
Even in his casual clothes, he always managed to look devastating. He caught her look and smiled.

Valerie looked away hastily, and opened her briefcase.
She felt acutely conscious of his presence—and awkward
about it. Here she was, sitting around a conference table
with members of the board and other teachers—with a
board member she'd spent a lot of time with. With a board
member she'd kissed.

She felt her cheeks warming, and continued to shuffle
through the papers in her briefcase, finally withdrawing a
pad of paper and pen.

Bernie began and they went through a few formalities,
running through the minutes from the last meeting. Then
Bernie handed out the teachers' new list of demands.

They'd made some strides, Valerie thought. They'd
dropped their demand for a 10% raise the first year to
9.5%—not much, she realized, but at least it was something. Their team planned to stand firm on that for now.
But they'd also dropped their demand for an extra sick day,
leaving it at the usual ten sick days per year. They had
recognized it was unlikely the board would give in on that,
and decided to drop the demand as a show of good faith.
They hoped the board would see it as a genuine concession.

Bernie went over their changes, and Valerie tried to
study Douglas without being obvious. He was reading over
the demands.

She watched the others too. Most of the board members
wore neutral expression. Mr. Tyler wore a frown. He turned
to the lawyer, and whispered something. Then he requested
a caucus.

Already? Valerie thought, as the board left the room.

Their team milled around, talking. Al and Jim both looked uneasy.

Anne asked her about the situation with Scarlett.

"I'm going to have to talk to her mother or father," Valerie said. "Her behavior's getting worse."

The board returned shortly. Mr. Tyler announced in a superior tone that the board found these new demands unacceptable. But, he said, they had made some concessions of their own, and passed out the new document.

Valerie skimmed over the board's new proposal with a sinking heart. The board was offering a 1% pay raise—ridiculous! It was almost as insulting as offering no raise at all. And they were still demanding that the teachers pay their own insurance! She gritted her teeth so she wouldn't make a disparaging sound.

The only positive note in the entire package was that the board had agreed that the teachers were entitled to a bereavement day off in the case of the death of a grandparent.

She looked up to see Bernie looking intently at each one of the team in turn.

Then he asked for a caucus.

Once back in the faculty room, Al began groaning about the board's being so rigid.

"Well, they gave in on the grandparents' death day," Phyllis pointed out.

"But they're still asking us to pay our own insurance costs!" he exclaimed.

"They did come up since last time," Bernie stated. "More than we went down."

"Our members will never agree to paying for their medical insurance," Valerie said.

"I think they're using it as a negotiations ploy," Anne suggested.

"I agree," Bernie said. "I wouldn't get too upset about it—not yet, anyway." He stuck his hands in his pockets.

"How can we not?" Al grumbled.

They returned to the conference room. Valerie found her

nerves had tightened, and wondered if she looked as grim as she felt.

She couldn't help it. She had hoped that this session of negotiations would go smoothly. Partly, she admitted to herself, because she hoped that maybe, just maybe, Douglas' perceptions about the teachers had changed since he'd spent time with her. And that he'd be able to influence the board to be more reasonable.

It didn't look like that had happened.

Bernie spoke first, expressing regret that the board hadn't tried harder to meet the teachers' requests. Mr. Tyler then spoke, in formal terms, claiming that they had bent over backwards to meet the union's unreasonable demands. Valerie felt annoyance at the condescending way Marvin Tyler spoke, but kept her mouth shut. Bernie has warned them not to express anger—at least not so early in the negotiations process. But it was difficult. She sneaked a quick look at Douglas. His face was calm, his expression implacable.

It seemed he was in agreement with the rest of the board.

Discouragement began to creep through her system.

The meeting ended shortly, with an agreement on the next date for all of them.

Valerie got up slowly. She lifted her briefcase, and, feeling as if she was being watched, glanced around.

Douglas was studying her.

Uncomfortable with his scrutiny, she glanced away, and followed Phyllis out of the room.

Once home, she played with her cats, then decided to take a nice warm bath. She heard the phone ring while she was in the tub, and let the answering machine pick it up. When she came out, wrapped in her old, comfortable blue terry robe, she saw no messages.

Whoever it was had hung up without leaving a message.

She gave into temptation and dialed "*69."

It was Douglas' phone number.

*   *   *

"Miss McFadden, he took my pencil," Dustin whined, pointing to Jason, another student.

"Did not!" Jason protested.

"Did too," Dustin declared.

"Shut up," mumbled Curtis, beside Dustin.

Valerie sighed and stood up. "First, let's check your desk to see if it's there," she said to Dustin. He had a habit of misplacing things.

The pencil was not there, although there were plenty of markers and crumpled papers in the desk. Dustin and Jason began bickering.

"That's enough," Valerie said firmly. How much time til gym class? she wondered. This morning had dragged. Maybe it was the rainy weather, but the class seemed hyperactive and disagreeable today. The break would be a good thing for all of them. She tried to sound as patient as usual. "I want this fighting to stop, now. Dustin, you'll have to take one of the pencils from my desk. That's your third one this week, I believe. We don't have an unlimited supply."

"I wouldn't need one if he hadn't took it—"

"I didn't!"

"Boys!" This time she didn't hide the sharp note, and the rest of the class looked up. "That's quite enough," she announced. "Go back to your seats and get back to work. I am getting annoyed now."

Glaring at each other, the boys resumed their seats.

Valerie kept a close eye on the two boys—and on Scarlett too. She had gotten nasty again yesterday—and this was after the guidance counselor had tried talking to her. Scarlett wasn't picking on anyone else, just Kayla, and Valerie suspected it was because Kayla got emotional and Scarlett knew she could get to her.

She had decided to call Scarlett's mother, Mrs. Smith, at work during the students' gym class this morning, to see if she could get her to speak to Scarlett about her behavior.

When the class finally went to gym, she went into the guidance office and found a quiet corner to make the call. After introducing herself—Scarlett's mother hadn't appeared on back-to-school night—she explained the problem.

"I'm a very busy woman," Scarlett's mother snapped. "I have a demanding managerial job here at MacLellan Crackers. I work long hours. I don't have time to deal with these stupid little problems. It's your classroom. It's your problem."

Valerie had been prepared for the woman's negative attitude—she'd heard about her from several faculty members—but hadn't expected it to be quite so abrasive. She swallowed, and said in a reasonable tone, "Of course it's my problem. But it's Scarlett's too, and I want you to be aware of it. I'm hoping that we can keep this from getting out of hand. It really hurts this other girl's feelings when she calls her things like a hen."

"Well, she is," the woman retorted. "It's not Scarlett's fault that the girl is heavy."

Valerie sat back, shocked. Well. It seemed that Scarlett must be following her mother's example of making insulting remarks. Mrs. Smith sounded like a real snob. Valerie let a distinct edge creep into her voice. "Nonetheless, in my classroom I do *not* tolerate name-calling. We respect each other as individuals."

"How nice." There was no mistaking the woman's sarcasm.

"Tell me, do you think this kind of childish behavior would be tolerated in the corporate world?" There was a second of silence, and Valerie pushed on. "You work for a large international company, Mrs. Smith, and you come into contact with many, many people. I'm sure in a corporate environment it's an advantage to get along with the different people employed there, even people who you dislike—who might be your superiors. You can't get ahead in that kind of company with childish behavior. It will be a lot better for Scarlett if she learns that at a young age, rather than when she could lose a job because of a foolish remark." She found herself leaning forward as if Mrs. Smith was there in person, anxiously hoping her words would sink in. "You may think these things and say them at home, but I'm sure you'll agree this kind of remark has no place in a business environment."

She must have hit the right button, because there was a moment of silence.

"Well . . ." the woman said, a note of doubt in her voice.

Valerie continued, trying to sound reasonable and friendly yet firm while she had the mother's possible agreement. "I will talk to Scarlett again. Of course, she is only a child, and children do make mistakes—I just don't want to see this one happening over and over. It's better to stop it now. And I would greatly appreciated it if you could reinforce this at home. Perhaps you could talk to her about your job, and how important it is to have a good, professional attitude in the corporate world."

"If I have the time." Mrs. Smith still sounded snippy, but not quite as much.

"I appreciate it," Valerie said. "And I will call you in a week or so and let you know how things are going. And thank you for taking the time to speak with me," she finished graciously, fighting off an impulse to gag. She'd been lucky to get a few precious minutes of the woman's time. It was obvious Mrs. Smith thought she had far better things to do.

"Alright. Goodbye," the other woman said abruptly, and hung up.

Valerie sat back, drained. Would her call make a difference? Would Scarlett's mother take the time to speak with her? She'd better make a plan in case she didn't. Although the woman had sounded better at the end of their conversation, there was no guarantee she'd speak to Scarlett. And it was quite obvious that Scarlett was emulating her mother when she made these nasty comments.

Well, she might not be able to change Scarlett's behavior at home. But she was certainly not going to allow her to behave badly in class.

Sighing, Valerie got up and went to correct some papers.

When her class came back from gym, they had expended some energy, and weren't quite as wound up as before. But she was glad that it was almost lunch time. A half hour in the faculty room would be a good break. Between her class and the conversation with Mrs. Smith, Valerie was feeling out of sorts.

But as she opened the door to the faculty room, she was struck by a raised voice: "—pay our own insurance!" The whining voice belonged to Sam, a fifth grade teacher in his early fifties who was a constant complainer. Oh no, she thought, more whining. Just what she needed. "I've never heard of such a thing in all the years I've been teaching. They've got nerve!"

Shanna was already seated at one end of the table, and waved at Valerie. Valerie raised her eyebrows and went to get her lunch from the refrigerator.

"And offering a one percent pay raise?" asked Paula, the art teacher. "It's demeaning."

Sam was shaking his head. "The board's getting worse and worse," he said gloomily. "When was the last time any of those guys got pay raises at their jobs? I bet it was a lot more than one percent!"

Valerie tried not to pay attention as Sam droned on and on. She took out her lunch, got a diet soda from the machine, and sat down next to Shanna.

"Are you coming to aerobics this afternoon?" Shanna asked.

They tried to go a few times a week, and Valerie thought today would be a perfect day to work out. Maybe she'd get rid of some of her tension. "Yes," she said.

Ruby, dressed in a bright red and gold pants outfit, entered the room, smiling widely. Valerie indicated the seat on her other side.

"What was the team's reaction to all this?" asked Henry, a mild-mannered man in his fifties, when Sam paused.

The group turned to look at Valerie.

"We're angry," Valerie began. She had to be careful—there was no sense in stirring things up prematurely. They'd only had two negotiating sessions. "But it's early in the negotiating process, so we don't want to get too militant yet—"

"Don't ask her," Sam interrupted in an insulting tone. "She's going soft."

Chapter Nine

V alerie stared at Sam in astonishment. "*Soft*? What on earth do you mean?" Her stomach clenched. She had a bad feeling about this.

Anne was entering the faculty room with several more teachers behind her as Sam spoke. She came to Valerie's defense immediately. "That's not true," she exclaimed.

Sam now had the attention of everyone in the room. "I mean now that you're hanging around with your fancy Board of Ed friend," he continued loudly.

Valerie felt like she was slowly submerging in icy water.

"I saw you," Sam accused, "at Olson's Farm on Saturday, having a grand old time picking pumpkins and cozying up to the new board member."

Someone gasped.

For a moment Valerie stared at Sam, unable to think of a thing to say. He'd seen her? *With Douglas*? There was a moment of silence. It was as if everyone in the room was holding their breaths, waiting to hear what she would say.

"And Kurt said you two were looking mighty tight at the happy hour," Sam continued.

On the heels of her consternation came genuine anger. Sam, of all people, implying she had connections to the Board of Ed! "You have a lot of nerve," Valerie said, slowly and emphatically. She raised her voice just a notch. "Accusing me of having board connections. We all know you got your job here—at a time when teaching jobs were

108

hard to find—because your godfather was on the board of education."

"That was a coincidence!" Sam denied hotly. "I graduated with honors and was well qualified for the job—"

"His uncle, actually," Mary Dolan said implacably, taking a spoonful of soup. The white-haired woman had taught for many years. She sent Valerie a quick smile. "And if I had the chance to go out with a man as handsome and charming as Douglas Cooper, I'd take it in a heartbeat."

"So would I," Ruby said firmly. She was never one to be quiet. "That's her personal business," she continued, rounding on Sam. "Not yours."

"It affects us all!" Sam exclaimed.

"Wait a minute." Anne was using the tone she used when her class misbehaved. She sent Valerie a quick, encouraging look, then stared at Sam. "This kind of fighting won't get us anywhere."

Valerie's fingers were still gripping her sandwich bag tightly. "You're right," she declared. "In fact, I'm sure the Board of Ed would like to see us fighting among ourselves. It would make our union weaker, and it's a lot harder to negotiate when we're not united!"

She paused. People were still staring.

"As far as my acquaintance with Douglas Cooper, there's nothing to hide. He's raising his niece and nephew because his brother and sister-in-law were killed in a car accident. I went on an outing with all of them. I am not going soft." She said it firmly.

Sam had one parting comment. "We'll see." He said it in an almost threatening manner. With that he left the room, slamming the door.

"Well, isn't he in a snit," Ruby said loudly, seating herself beside Valerie.

"Nothing unusual," Anne agreed, taking the seat on Ruby's other side.

"Don't pay any attention to Sam," Shanna said encouragingly. "He needs to get a life!"

But Valerie's three friends were also giving her looks which suggested there'd be a lot more questions later, when all the other faculty members weren't around.

Valerie wanted to groan. She hadn't said anything to anyone about Douglas, except to her friend Karen, who lived far away. A little worried about just such a reaction, she'd kept silent. Now her girlfriends would want to know why—and want to know every single detail of their relationship.

"What's the weather report for tomorrow?" Henry asked.

"Rain for the next couple of days," Anne replied.

People began talking, some in low-pitched voices, some louder. Valerie heard the words "Board of Ed" and "negotiations."

On the opposite side of the table, Mary Dolan winked at her.

Douglas finished going over the accountant's monthly report and put it aside. The annual Labor Day Sale last month had been one of their best. Business was good.

He glanced out the window. Heavy rain slanted down, drumming on the blacktop. It was a pleasant sound, almost soothing.

Thursday was his day to work late. Sean and/or Jessica would meet the children at his house and take care of them until he got home. Riley, who loved to curl up and sleep on gray days like this, hadn't even wanted to come to work with him. When he'd left the house at noon, she'd been sound asleep on the family room couch.

Thursday . . . and tomorrow was Friday.

He'd see Valerie again.

She had been constantly in his thoughts all week, and he found it astounding. He rarely thought so much about a woman. He certainly hadn't given Hillary this much thought, even when they were spending a lot of time together. It must be, he concluded, because he hadn't dated lately.

Not because Valerie was beautiful. Or fun to be with. Or compassionate and warm.

Not because kissing her was a dream.

He stretched, and was about to file the papers when there was a knock on his door. "Yes?"

Sean poked his head in. "Carl Warren's here to see you. Are you busy?"

Surprised, Douglas shook his head. "No, I can see him."

Mr. Warren entered the room. He wore a suit and tie and Douglas guessed he'd just come from his job at the bank.

"Hi, Carl," Douglas said, and they shook hands.

"Good to see you, Douglas. The place is booming." He gave his rather stiff smile. "I'm glad business is good, and you and your cousin are keeping up the family traditions."

"Have a seat," Douglas invited. As the older man sat down, Douglas did too.

Mr. Warren asked after his parents, uncle and aunt, and they spoke for a few minutes about them, and about his niece and nephew. Small talk, but Douglas suspected there was something else on the man's mind.

"I heard you've been seeing someone," Carl said after a couple of minutes. "It's time you thought about settling down, Douglas. You must be—what—about thirty?"

"Almost thirty-one," Douglas corrected. What the heck did he mean, seeing someone? He couldn't mean—

"Well, that young chick on the negotiating team is a real looker," Carl continued. "What's her name—Miss Mc-Fadden?"

Douglas was astonished. He hadn't told anyone except Sean and Jessica about dating Valerie, and they certainly weren't gossips. How did Carl Warren know?

His surprise must have shown on his face, because Carl continued, "You know how word gets around in small towns like ours." He chuckled.

"Yes. But we're not really seeing each other, not the way you mean—"

"Oh, I know you young people don't jump into marriage

the way my generation did," Carl said with a wave. "But your going out with her should give us a real 'in' as to what the teachers are thinking, what strategies they're planning to use." He grinned. "Not that I think that's the only reason you're dating her," he added, as he watched Douglas. "She's a beautiful woman. But it could certainly be to our advantage to have you scoping out the opposite side, so to speak."

Douglas felt anger begin to simmer in his gut. "I'm not dating her for her looks," he said slowly. "She happens to be a very nice, very warm person. And I'm certainly not dating her so I can do any spying. I wouldn't use her—or anyone—that way."

"Well, I wouldn't call it spying," Carl said, making Douglas wonder what exactly he *would* call it. "But if you keep your eyes and ears open, I'm sure you can find out a thing or two," Carl went on.

Douglas didn't want to hear another word. "Forget it, Carl," he said flatly. "I have no intentions of doing anything of the kind."

Carl stared at him for a second. "So you are serious about her," he drawled.

Serious? Was he kidding? "No," Douglas protested. "I'm not serious."

But Carl just smiled. "You're awfully quick to jump to her defense. Okay, forget I suggested it."

"I will forget it," Douglas said, fighting to keep his tone civil. What Carl was suggesting was that he use Valerie! Which he would never do.

Carl got up. "Good luck then."

"I'm not serious," Douglas repeated.

Carl shook hands and left. But there was a satisfied look on his face.

Douglas stared at the closed door when he left.

He would never take Carl's "spying" suggestion. That was so sneaky, so despicable to him, it wasn't even worth thinking about. Carl should never have suggested such a thing.

As to his other suggestion . . . Well, maybe he and Valerie had gone out a few times. Maybe you could even consider it dating. But serious? He hadn't given thought to getting serious. He wanted to spend time with Valerie, get to know her better, simply to be with her.

For the first time, he wondered what Valerie's thoughts on the subject were.

Carefully balancing her umbrella and the shopping bag full of ingredients, Valerie walked through the rain up the walk to Douglas' house.

The dark red Victorian was three-stories high, and charming. In the dark, rainy late afternoon, light spilled from its windows and it seemed to welcome her with open arms.

She'd had a lot of misgivings since Thursday about coming here. It hadn't helped that Wednesday Shanna had questioned her incessantly at aerobics, not to mention the calls she'd had from Ruby and Anne that night. Everyone wanted to know about her relationship with Douglas. But despite her misgivings she would never disappoint the children. So right after school she'd finished correcting papers, zipped home, played with the cats, fed them, and changed to jeans and a sweater. Then she'd gathered up the ingredients she'd bought last night, and driven through the dark afternoon to Douglas' home. Before she could ring the doorbell, however, excited barking started from the other side of the door.

"Okay, Riley." She could hear Douglas, and then the door opened. "Hi Valerie! C'mon in."

He took her umbrella and bag as a black and tan dog frolicked about her.

"Hello!" she said. "And who are you?" she greeted the dog.

The dog gave a happy snort and jumped on her, wagging its tail like mad.

"Whoa, Riley. Give her a chance to get to know you before you knock her over," Douglas said, pulling the dog down.

"It's okay, I love dogs," Valerie said, and bent to pet the dog. "Aren't you beautiful! What kind is she?" she asked as Riley licked her hand.

"A mix—Lab, Rotweiller, and some kind of hound," he said.

She straightened, and before she realized what was happening, Douglas bent toward her and gave her a quick kiss on the lips. Even that abbreviated kiss sent tingling straight down to Valerie's toes.

"I'll take your jacket," Douglas said as Lindsay appeared.

"Hi Valerie!" she said, smiling widely. Her hair was pulled into a ponytail with a scrunchie and she wore jeans and an orange top decorated with a witch, with the words "Happy Halloween" in black.

"Hi," Valerie said, smiling. She noted there was a plastic pumpkin by the foot of the stairs, and was glad she'd worn her Halloween vest with her long-sleeved orange T-shirt and jeans. She liked to get in the mood of the holiday along with her students.

"We're all ready!" Lindsay announced. She tugged on Valerie's hand. "I'll show you the kitchen."

Valerie laughingly followed her down the hall into a large, comfortable yellow kitchen with mellow wood cabinets and lots of counter space. In the middle of the kitchen table sat the pumpkins the children had picked. Instead of carving them, they had painted faces on them. Matt's was scary and Lindsay's pretty. "I'd love a tour later," she said as Douglas followed them.

Lindsay opened a door and yelled down, "Matt! Valerie's here!"

The dog played around Valerie, jumping and smiling.

Matt bounded up the stairs, also dressed in jeans and a Spiderman sweatshirt. Douglas had brought in her bag of ingredients and placed it on the table.

"Hi," Matt said, more subdued than Lindsay but still smiling.

"I brought some Halloween music," Valerie said. "Do you have a CD player?"

"A portable, over there," Douglas said, pointing to the corner of the counter. "What's this? Spooky Halloween music?" he read from the label.

"My classes always love this tape. I bring it to the Halloween party every year," Valerie told him. "It's got things like the theme from the 'Twilight Zone' and 'Ghostbusters'."

"Cool!" Matt remarked.

She laid out the ingredients while Douglas brought out the utensils they would need. She quickly had the children involved in breaking eggs, adding sugar and canned pumpkin.

Douglas stayed around, and as the music blared they all took turns stirring. Once the cookies were on the sheets, they added the chocolate and orange sprinkles she'd brought, and drew faces with premade chocolate icing. Douglas got into the act and they were soon trying to outdo each other with funny and scary cookies. While they worked, Valerie found herself more comfortable and relaxed working in close proximity to Douglas, than she had expected to be.

Once the cookies were in the oven, they all cleaned up, and then the children drifted off, Lindsay to play with her dolls and Matt to watch TV.

"I'll give you the tour when the cookies come out of the oven," Douglas promised. "And I'll order a couple of pizzas. What kind do you like?"

They talked for a few minutes while Valerie played with Riley. Once the cookies were cooling, Douglas guided her around the house.

The house was charming and bigger than some other Victorians Valerie had been in. It had a large living room, dining room and kitchen, and a small family room and den on the first floor. Douglas had turned the smallest den into a home office, complete with a large desk, a new computer, and bookcases.

The basement playroom he had worked on was large, with some old furniture, a comfortable couch, and a TV where the children had a Playstation and DVD player hooked up. He'd also put his old computer down there with some games, he explained, for the kids to fool around with. "Although they do use my new computer for homework," he told her.

Upstairs there were five bedrooms. The children and Douglas used three of them, and one, which had been Keith's, he explained with a touch of sadness, was now a TV room. The fifth had been turned into a guestroom. "For when my parents visit," he added.

The house had some substantial and old features, like the big fireplace in the living room, sliding doors that came out of the wall in the dining room to separate it from the living room, and wooden molding throughout. The whole effect was warm and welcoming.

"It's a wonderful house," Valerie said. "You must love it here."

As they walked around, Douglas placed his hand lightly on her shoulder a couple of times, and without the children crowding around, Valerie was back to being acutely conscious of every move he made. Of every little touch and look.

When the pizza arrived, they all sat down at the kitchen table. Dinner was cheerful, with the kids talking about their day at school and making plans for Halloween, and how much candy they'd accumulate.

As they sat in the warm kitchen, talking and laughing, it struck Valerie how comfortable the four of them were.

Almost, she thought, like a family.

But that was a dangerous thought.

After dinner, Douglas fed Riley dog food mixed with some pizza scraps, which she devoured happily, and then took her for a walk. Valerie collected her things. "You're not leaving so soon?" he asked upon his return.

"Well, I . . ." Valerie hesitated.

Matthew had come into the room. "Aren't you going to read us one of those ghost stories?" he asked. "I saw the book in your bag." She'd brought along the old book of spooky stories, from which she would select a few to read to her class as a reward for good behavior the week of Halloween.

Valerie had to admit she was glad for an excuse to stay. She really was enjoying herself. "Okay."

They went into the family room and she read them the stories about the lady who vanished from a car and the haunted picture of a castle in Scotland. They begged for another, so she read them the old legend of the talking cats from the Catskills in upstate New York.

"Will you tuck me in and read me a story when it's time to go to sleep?" Lindsay asked suddenly. "Please?" The little girl looked at her hopefully.

Her expression tugged at Valerie's heart, and a lump formed in Valerie's throat. She swallowed, and looked at Douglas. She saw an entreating look on his face too.

"Okay," she agreed.

"Lindsay and Matt get to stay up later on Fridays and Saturdays," he explained. "In half an hour, Lindsay, you should get ready for bed."

"Okay," Lindsay said with a brilliant smile.

While the children watched a favorite Friday night comedy, with Riley snoozing nearby, Douglas and Valerie sat in the living room. They talked about his house, and their families. "So how come you never got married?" Douglas asked abruptly, and Valerie wondered if he'd been planning to ask that question.

She sighed. "I came close once—at least, I thought I was

coming close." She settled back in the couch and crossed her arms. "I was crazy about Stuart," she went on. "He was fun and friendly, and smart. But he had no intention of getting married, ever. His parents had a very bitter divorce and he had decided he'd never marry. His goal in life was to play the field, and go from one woman to another." Now her voice took on an acerbic note. "I wanted marriage and a family. I refused to date him indefinitely, until he decided to go on to someone else. So we broke up."

"You did the right thing," Douglas said, surprising her. "You knew what you wanted and that things wouldn't work with him."

"Yes, well, it was painful." Valerie looked away.

There was an awkward silence. Valerie's thoughts sped around. Are you like Stuart? she wanted to ask. Douglas had said he wasn't sure he'd get married—he already had a family. Did that mean he never wanted anything more? Or he hadn't given it much thought?

It was on the tip of her tongue to ask.

Instead, she said, dryly, "It sounds like your Hillary and Stuart would have deserved each other."

"Yeah." Douglas gave a brief smile. He glanced at his watch. "I see it's already past Lindsay's bedtime. I must have lost track of time."

She had a feeling he was avoiding further discussion of this topic.

She stood up. "I'll tuck her in," she said.

Lindsay protested only slightly about going to sleep. She got ready for bed, and when Valerie went up to her pink and purple room, she already had a book out.

"This is my favorite story," she said, handing Valerie a worn copy of *Grimm's Fairy Tales.* The one she had it open to was "The Twelve Dancing Princesses."

"I always liked that story too!" Valerie said, and read her the story, in an appropriately dramatic voice.

She was surprised when Matt also came into the room and flopped down on the bed in companionable silence. He was followed by Riley, who curled up in a corner, and then Douglas, who slid silently into the room and sat down on the floor.

She continued reading, concentrating on the story and not her listeners. When she finished, Lindsay applauded, and Douglas and Matt joined in.

"That was great," Lindsay said with a sigh.

"Another fairy tale about the beautiful princess and the handsome prince-in-disguise," Douglas said in a teasing voice.

"They're fun stories," Valerie started to protest.

"I wasn't criticizing," Douglas said. "Just observing. I know people enjoy those tales. They've been around for over 100 years." He looked at Lindsay. "Ever hear the one about the twelve sword-fighting pirates?"

"There is no such story," Matt scoffed.

"Oh, yes, there is," Douglas said, and proceeded to make one up.

Valerie had to admit it was pretty funny for a spontaneously created story. Soon Douglas had them laughing as he tried to make up a story similar to a Grimm Brothers' fairytale.

When he finished—a ridiculous ending, in which the pirates conquered the enchanted sea and danced off into the night with the twelve maidens they rescued—he ruffled Lindsay's hair and gave her a quick kiss. "Time for sleep."

The left the room, leaving the night light on, the door open and the hall light on too. Douglas whispered that Lindsay liked a lot of lights on when she first went to sleep, ever since her parents died. Valerie nodded.

"I turn the lights off when I go to sleep," he finished. "But the night light stays on all night." He turned to Matt. "Time for you to go to sleep too."

Matt was almost ready, and they tucked him in. Valerie didn't think a nine year old boy would want a kiss, so she merely hugged him, and Douglas patted his shoulder.

Riley followed them down the stairs and into the hall.

"I guess I'd better get going," Valerie said.

"Not yet," Douglas said.

Before she could move or speak he pulled her into his arms and kissed her.

Electricity zinged through her as Douglas's arms surrounded her. She was totally aware of his warm lips crushing hers, of the searing power of his kiss. Every molecule in her responded, and all thoughts drained away. Vaguely, she thought she heard something. Maybe it was her own sigh against his mouth. His hands caressed her back.

He lifted his head just slightly, whispered, "Valerie," and kissed her again.

Her bones were melting.

And then, she heard something again. A giggle, followed by a scampering sound.

One of the kids. Or both.

She stepped back and Douglas loosened his hold. His eyes were bright, and his expression dazed.

The kiss was affecting him as well.

Something flared inside of her.

"I—better go," she said, feeling a little dazed herself.

He cupped her chin. "Okay. Drive carefully."

"Of course." She gathered her things together, and he walked her out.

The rain had ceased, and the night was crisply cool and clear. A wind had sprung up, and felt good against her hot cheeks. Leaning against the car, he placed a hand on her shoulder: "I want to see you again," he said simply. "I'll call you in a few days."

"Okay," she whispered. She got into the car, waved at Douglas, and drove away.

She opened the window of her car as she drove, letting in the delicious fall air. Fall, her favorite season, she thought for the thousandth time. Pumpkins, gorgeous leaves, Halloween.

Falling in love.

A lightning bolt of excitement shot through her.

Followed by a wave of trepidation.

Because she was afraid that, during this most beautiful of the seasons, she was falling in love with Douglas Cooper.

But was he falling in love with her? And if he did . . . then what?

She couldn't help thinking thoughts about forever.

Chapter Ten

Douglas found himself whistling as he strolled back into the house. A strange feeling surrounded him. A feeling divided into even parts of satisfaction and frustration. He was satisfied because he'd been so happy during the last few hours. They'd flown by.

Yet there was also frustration. He'd have liked more time alone with Valerie. A lot more time, he had to admit.

The wonderful aroma of home-baked cookies, laced with subtle spices, assailed him. He inhaled deeply. What had Valerie put in the dough? Sugar and flour, cinnamon and nutmeg. He closed the door and heard a slight scampering. And he didn't think it was mice.

Ha. He'd been right. It was the children. They'd been spying on him and Valerie.

He bounded up the stairs. Riley met him at the top. She must have run up to see what the kids were doing!

"Okay, I know you're not sleeping," he boomed out.

Lindsay giggled.

Matt appeared at his bedroom doorway. "Hey."

"Do you want to tell me what you guys were doing out of bed?" Douglas said, keeping his voice mild. He was tempted to laugh. It was obvious what they'd been doing.

Lindsay materialized from her doorway. "Spying on you," she said frankly. And giggled again.

"I thought so," Douglas said. "But it's really not nice. A guy wants to have some privacy with his girlfriend."

"So she *is* your girlfriend," Matt said wisely.

Douglas realized it had slipped out. "Well, I guess, kind of," he said. He sounded like he was about Matt's age, he thought ruefully.

"Are you going to marry Valerie?" Lindsay asked eagerly.

"Whoa, you're going too fast for me," Douglas said, putting out his hands.

Riley sat down, waving her tail, and looked up at him. It seemed even she was interested in this conversation.

"Why not? She's cool," Matt declared.

And that, Douglas was aware, was very high praise from a nine-year-old.

"I know that," he said gravely, fighting to keep a straight face.

"We could use a mother," Lindsay added.

He stared at his niece. That had never occurred to him. He shoved his hands in his pockets. "You think so?"

Two heads nodded at him.

"Well, I'll consider it," he said slowly. "Now back to bed."

They dashed back to their rooms, and he heard Lindsay giggle again.

He returned downstairs, Riley at his heels. He settled down in the family room, and turned the TV on. And stared at it blankly while the dog curled up on the opposite corner of the couch.

He had thought that he had an instant family. He had thought he didn't really need a wife. But he hadn't given thought to the fact that the kids might need—and want—a mother.

Even if they did, however, and even if he wanted a wife, would Valerie fit the role?

Yes, she was friendly and warm and compassionate. She was great with kids too. And she certainly was beautiful. But he knew marriage needed more than that. He continued to sit there, thinking, for a long time.

* * *

Valerie tumbled into bed and slept late the next morning, her sleep full of hopeful dreams. When she woke, she was full of energy and tackled her apartment. She'd started on Thursday and now finished in a frenzy of cleaning. Then she ran errands, including getting some new toys for King and Cleo. When she returned it was just after two in the afternoon. She took a quick shower, grabbed the paperback book she'd bought at last week's garage sale, and settled down on the couch to read while the cats played nearby.

She felt surprisingly good. Her future might be unsure, negotiations might be precarious, and yet, the air seemed to sparkle.

It was because of Douglas.

She stretched, and was about to open her book when she noticed the answering machine was blinking. She rewound it. The first message was from Shanna. She'd gotten Valerie's message yesterday about getting together for the movies, but as it turned out one of her high school friends was coming out for the day. But, she added, they'd get to the movies one of these days.

The second was from Anne, asking if Valerie wanted to come over that evening. Tony was visiting his brother for the weekend and she planned to rent a couple of videos, and watch them after her son went to sleep. Did Valerie want to join her?

The third message had her reeling, almost falling off the couch in shock.

"Hello, Valerie," said a voice she instantly recognized. "This is Stuart. I really need to talk to you. Can you call?" He gave his phone number, which had the area code for northeastern New Jersey.

She was so shocked she had to rewind the message and play it two more times.

Stuart? *Stuart?* Calling her?

Why?

He'd sounded more subdued than he had five years ago. Less carefree.

What on earth did he want to speak to her about?

She reached for the phone and dialed the number he'd left.

"Hi," said the once familiar voice.

"Stuart?" Valerie's voice sounded squeaky.

There was some static, and music in the background. "Hold on," he said. "I'm on my cell in a store." She heard movement, and the music faded. "Okay, that should be better," he said. "I'm going back to my car. How are you?"

"Fine. And you?" she asked coolly. Her insides were churning. Her last conversation with Stuart had been their final break-up, and she'd walked away with a broken heart. Did he really expect she'd be glad to hear from him?

"I know you probably think it's strange to hear from me," he said. "But I've been thinking about you for months, babe."

"Don't call me that," she snapped, the words automatic. Babe! He had to be kidding!

"Listen, I really need to talk to you. Can we get together later today? I'm in Hoboken. I could be there in say, an hour and a half, two hours."

"No." That was automatic too. "Whatever you want to talk about we can talk about on the phone."

There was an audible sigh. "I was afraid you'd say that. Hold on, let me get in my car." More noises. Then it grew quieter. "Can't say I blame you," Stuart said, his voice still rather cheerful. "I was a jerk the last time you saw me."

She wasn't going to deny that. But her first reaction of anger was being replaced by something else . . . confusion.

She waited in silence, and after a moment, he went on. "Listen, Valerie. I . . . life's had its ups and downs in the last few years. And for the last few months you've been on my mind. A lot. There's no one quite like you," he said, and his voice dropped.

She waited for him to go on. Wild thoughts that he might be dying, or in need of money, or hiding out from the mob bounced through her head. Why was he calling?

"And?" she prompted.

"And I was thinking you were right all along. There are some real advantages to marriage. And I'd like to start seeing you again."

Shock pulsed through her. Stuart talking about marriage? Stuart wanting to see her again?

"I made a mistake." His voice was unexpectedly humble. "I want you back, babe."

She was so surprised she didn't even order him to stop calling her babe. She sat back, gripping the phone so tightly it dug into her fingers.

Her thoughts swirled. Stuart wanted her back. It was what she had wanted, long ago.

But Stuart had proved how selfish and uncaring he was. And although she had been hurt, she had realized later that she was better off without someone like that. She had no reason to believe otherwise now.

Had he really thought he could stroll back into her life and resume their relationship? Did he really have the colossal ego to think she'd welcome him with open arms?

Anger resurfaced, this time cold and controlled.

"You want me back?" Her voice was tight. "What on earth makes you think I want you?"

"You may not—at least not right now." Another sigh. "I deserve this, I know. I broke your heart. But I'm changed, babe. I'm willing to show you and make amends." His voice was softly persuasive. "Can we meet?"

"No. Not today." She definitely didn't want to see Stuart today. Maybe never.

"Okay, then some other time? Please?"

"I don't think—"

He interrupted. "Val, babe, I know I hurt you. I know you have good reason to think you hate me. But you loved me once." His words came faster. "I've changed, I really have. And I realized that no other woman out there is as caring as you. I want another chance."

"I—" it was on the tip of her tongue to say she'd met someone else. But her love life was certainly not Stuart's business. He'd lost any claim to knowing about her personal life long ago. Still, she felt some curiosity. Had he really changed that much?

"Look, I can't meet you tonight," she said. "I have plans."

"Cancel them," he said silkily. "For me."

"No way," she retorted. She was not about to go running to Stuart, even if she had no plans!

"Fine, I can accept that." Just a shade of arrogant forbearance crept into his voice, and Valerie found herself gritting her teeth. How dare he act like he was the injured party?

"Give me one good reason why I should ever see you again," she ground out.

"Because I've realized I'm wrong."

She waited. He was silent.

Finally, she spoke. "I'll think about it." She certainly wasn't going to jump at the chance to see Stuart after five years. And yet, some curiosity wound through her. Had he really changed? "I'll think about seeing you," she repeated. "And call you in a few days."

He sighed. "Please call me."

"Alright," she said. "Goodbye." And she clicked off the phone before he could say anything else.

Stuart. Calling her.

Once she would have been joyful to think he'd changed and wanted her back. Now she was suspicious—had he really changed that much? Did he really think he wanted marriage?

Her feelings about Stuart were . . . well, not precisely non-existent. But she certainly didn't love him, not anymore. And she doubted that would change.

And what about Douglas?

She did love Douglas. Of that she was positive.

But the fact remained that Douglas might be another Stuart. Could she go through that again—loving a man who didn't want to commit?

She stared out the window, barely seeing the lovely fall day. The sun was shining, some fat clouds skidded across the sky, and a wind had sprung up and was rattling the window slightly.

The phone rang again. She refused to pick it up. She was not ready to speak to Stuart again so soon.

The answering machine picked up, and after a moment, started recording: "Hi Valerie . . ."

It was Douglas.

Douglas felt disappointment when Valerie's answering machine came on. He started to speak, when the machine suddenly stopped, and Valerie picked up.

"Oh, hi." She sounded a little out of breath. "Sorry, I couldn't pick the phone up right away."

"That's okay. Listen, I'd like to see you again." He'd gone over in his head what he planned to say. "How about dinner with me and the kids? Dinner out, this time," he added hastily. "Unless you prefer to eat in. The kids will be with us. Sean and Jessica are going out tonight and I'm not sure I can get a babysitter on short notice."

"Dinner? With the kids?" She sounded distracted. "Oh. Yes, that would be very nice." Now there was more enthusiasm in her voice. "I'd like that."

Warmth coursed through him. "What time is good for you?"

There was a pause. He imagined her looking at her watch and glanced at his own watch. It was just after three-thirty.

"Well, I know kids don't like to eat too late." She still sounded just a little flustered. "And the restaurants are really busy on Saturdays."

"We like the local diner a lot," he said. "Is that okay with you?"

"The Green Valley Diner? Oh, sure. Their food is delicious." She paused. "I guess . . . yes, I could be ready by five-thirty, and then we'd get there before the rush."

"Perfect." He smiled at Riley, who thumped her tail against the wood floor of his office. "I can pick you up. Or would you prefer to come here? Then you can hang out while the kids watch TV and . . . stay a while. I don't like to leave them for more than a few minutes—they're still young." How would she feel about spending the time with him, he wondered? Thinking of the kiss they'd shared yesterday, he waited, hoping she'd say yes, wanting that extra time with her, alone.

"I understand completely. They're too young to stay by themselves unless you're just running an errand." There was a pause. He pictured her on her couch, considering. "Okay, I'll come over around five-thirty."

He didn't realize he had been holding his breath until he heard her words. He let out a sigh of relief.

"I'll see you then. Bye." She hung up, sounding rushed.

He placed the cordless phone back in its cradle.

And stared out the window.

It was a nice fall day, with just a slight chill in the air. The sun was shining, and clouds moved across the sky. Douglas loved such days.

The sounds of laughter and running feet echoed through the house. Lindsay and Matt each had a friend over, and for a while they'd been watching a funny Halloween movie he'd bought them that week. The movie must have ended, because now he heard Lindsay saying something about getting out the Barbie dolls. And Matt and his friend were opening the basement door and clomping down the steps to the playroom—probably to play video games.

He could still smell the popcorn they'd been snacking on.

"C'mon, we'll check the family room. There's probably a few pieces lying around," he told Riley.

The dog followed him, tail wagging.

The kids had been good about leaving the bowls and

their empty soda cans in the kitchen, although there were a few pieces of popcorn scattered on the floor. Riley honed in on them at once. She was the only dog he'd ever had that liked popcorn, and he watched her with amusement for a moment.

The kids were great, and he loved them. Loved having them as his family. And the dog made it complete. If only they hadn't been his because of such tragic circumstances. But they were. And since last night, he'd been contemplating the fact that they were very possibly correct. They needed a mother.

And for the first time, he was aware of a certain gap in the picture. A gap in his own life.

His thoughts returned to Valerie.

Dinner with Douglas and the children was delightful.

Matt and Lindsay wanted to sit next to each other in the booth—were they matchmaking, Valerie wondered?—and got along beautifully, with only a minor squabble about who really liked French fries the most.

They talked about TV shows, books and general, non-controversial topics about school. And, of course, Halloween. Then the kids started talking about some Saturday morning cartoons, and Valerie got some time to speak to Douglas alone.

He was warm and charming and twice he touched her hand lightly.

And Valerie found herself sliding more and more into loving him.

Once they were back at Douglas' home, she played with Riley for a few minutes. The kids announced they were playing video games—now Valerie was pretty sure they were scheming to give her time alone with Douglas—and disappeared into the basement.

"Would you like a glass of wine or something else to drink?" Douglas asked.

"Just soda," Valerie said. She watched in amusement as

Douglas pushed aside juice packs, a gallon of milk and sports water bottles on the refrigerator shelf to get to the soda. Then he led the way into the living room.

"I noticed from some of your CDs you like jazz. I have the newest one by the Rippingtons—would you like to hear it?"

Valerie agreed, and watched as he took out the CD and slid it into the player. She was fully aware of being with him, even more so now that they were alone. She felt as if her nerves were taut, and as he sat beside her on the couch, she felt those same nerves were tingling. For a moment they just stared at each other.

"Valerie," Douglas whispered.

She gently touched his cheek as musical notes enveloped them.

And then he wrapped her in his arms, and kissed her, hard.

All the longing in Valerie welled up and she kissed him back, savoring the feel of his arms surrounding her, the pressure of his lips on hers. She would have been content to stay like that for years. She felt like she belonged there, in Douglas' arms. Forever.

It was Douglas who pulled away, just slightly, and gazed at her. Valerie's heart was racing, and the look she saw on his face made her heart jump.

A look of tenderness.

"Valerie," he whispered again, and smoothed her hair. "When I'm with you I want—I want to hold you, kiss you." He touched his forehead to hers, his lips barely a breath away. Brushing her lips softly, he whispered, "I feel like I could kiss you all night."

"Douglas . . ." she murmured. And reaching out, she pulled his head down again and kissed him back.

He held her tightly, and Valerie reveled in being in his arms, in the wonder and pleasure of his kiss.

She had never, ever experienced anything like this be-fore. She felt as if she sparkled, as if the whole night was lit up by their kiss. And she could stay like this forever, in his arms.

This was love.

After a few minutes Douglas loosened his grip on her, "I could keep doing this for hours. But I have to tell you I caught the kids spying on us last night."

Valerie felt her face grow warm. "You did?" There was a catch in her voice.

"Yes." He grinned suddenly. "They sneaked out of bed and I'm pretty sure they saw us kissing in the hall."

"Oh." For an instant, she couldn't think of a thing to say.

"It's not your fault," he added. "But we . . . we had a talk." He straightened, widening the distance between them.

"What did you say?" Valerie asked. Her breathing was still rapid, and she felt off-balance, almost dizzy, from the intensity of their kiss.

"I told them that a guy wants some privacy with his girlfriend."

Girlfriend! Valerie's heart started to dance. She smiled up at him. Placing her hand against his cheek, she asked, "And what did they say about that?"

"They said—" he hesitated, and she caught a look of uncertainty on his face. As if he wasn't quite sure how to put something into words. "They said that they could use a . . . mother."

"They could use a mother?" Valerie sat back, staring at him, as surprise reverberated through her system. The kids wanted a mother? Was that what this was all about? Wanting to see her, spend time with her—with the kids?

Her thoughts whirled as if tossed by an autumn wind. Did this mean Douglas was thinking that he might marry after all? That he did have a reason to get married? And were the children his *only* reason?

She must have stared blankly at him for a few seconds, because his forehead suddenly creased. "Valerie?" He still sounded unsure. "I—are you upset about the kids seeing us?"

"N-no," she said slowly. Somehow she had to pull her scattered thoughts together. "I mean—not very. But maybe our sitting here and—and kissing on the couch isn't such a good idea." Her voice trembled. *Maybe kissing you isn't such a good idea.* "At least, not now, not until I've sorted some of this out." She cleared her throat. "I'm just shocked by your comment. The other day you said something about not being sure you want to get married."

"I meant, I wasn't in a rush," he said. He raked a hand through his hair, and Valerie realized he was uncomfortable with this topic. "I'm not making myself very clear, am I? I mean, I've been thinking—maybe I *do* want to get married."

Maybe he wanted to get married. But as Valerie looked up at him, her heart slowly sank. Douglas was talking as if marriage was some kind of business deal. And maybe he did want marriage—but what about love?

"Do you believe in marriage without love?" she asked softly.

He stared at her, looking like he'd never given the idea any thought.

"I don't know," he said slowly. "I mean . . . heck, I don't know what I mean. Just that, well, they got me started thinking about marriage. Maybe I do want to get married."

But he sounded as confused as he looked. Valerie tried to smile, but was sure she looked stiff. "It sounds to me like you have some thinking to do," she said, gently.

He stared at her again, puzzlement in his eyes. "Yeah, maybe."

A noise and the creak of the basement door had Valerie pushing herself away from Douglas. "I better go. Before the kids start getting all kinds of ideas," she said.

Now Douglas looked surprised. Valerie rose, but her legs felt odd, almost shaky. Her heart was no longer dancing, and her thoughts seemed to have dropped all over the place. And she couldn't find them.

"Thank you for the evening," she said gravely.

"You're welcome." He got up, suddenly reached out and took her arm. "I want to see you, again, soon," he said, his voice dropping to a husky note.

There were footfalls in the hall.

"Okay," Valerie said, stepping back. "Soon."

She preceded him into the hall, where the two children, looking innocent and bright-eyed, lounged.

Despite her confusion, Valerie had to suppress a desire to laugh when she saw the two of them. They were trying so hard to look innocent, but it was clear they were very curious. "I have to get going," she told them. "But I'll see you soon." She smiled at them, then turned to smile at Douglas.

He was looking chagrinned. He sent the kids a look, then turned back to her. "I'll walk you to your car," he said.

Valerie hesitated. "Alright."

The night air was brisk and refreshing, and steadied her. Douglas draped his arm around her and they walked to her car.

"Thank you." Valerie didn't trust herself to say more. She needed to get home and get her thoughts and feelings sorted out.

"I'll see you soon." He leaned down to brush a kiss against her mouth.

Even that small gesture sent sparks shooting through her system.

Valerie waved when she got into her car, and drove away.

During the short ride home, she was mostly numb. But by the time she pulled into the driveway and the shared parking area in the back of the house, her thoughts were more coherent.

Douglas was thinking of marriage. An idea which she would have greeted with joy, except for one thing: he had said nothing about love. And as much as she loved him, as much as she could envision spending her life with him, she wanted him to love her right back. Just as much as she loved him.

She ran up the stairs and fitted her key into the lock.

And entering the apartment, she remembered Stuart's call.

Funny, she hadn't thought about Stuart all evening.

And that, she knew with clarity, meant she no longer cared about Stuart.

Oh, once she had. She'd thought she loved him—although now she wasn't sure that what she'd felt years ago had been love. It had been a much weaker emotion than what she was feeling now for Douglas. She definitely had never before experienced the kind of feelings that Douglas evoked in her.

She felt a spurt of laughter forming in her throat. How ironic, she thought, throwing her jacket off and curling up on the couch. Cleo jumped into her lap, and she cuddled the cat. Here she was with two men after her!

Stuart was repenting and said he was thinking about marriage, and that he still cared. And Douglas was thinking about marriage too . . . but maybe for the wrong reason.

She buried her face in Cleo's soft fur and felt rather than heard the cat's deep purr.

One man claimed to love her . . . and want marriage. But not the man she wanted.

The other wanted marriage . . . but perhaps for the wrong reason.

Monday was Columbus Day, and there was no school. Valerie met Shanna and Ruby at the mall and they shopped and ate lunch. She filled them in about what was going on with her, and Douglas. Both were supportive.

But that evening, alone in her apartment, she found herself torn between an intense desire to see Douglas again and the thought that perhaps it would be better if she didn't.

And what about Stuart?

Tuesday morning Valerie was glad to get into work and away from her ping-ponging thoughts. She was determined to concentrate on teaching and nothing else.

She was there early enough to have a leisurely cup of coffee in the faculty room. When she entered, she found a good-sized group already there.

Sam gave her a dour look as she approached the coffee-maker. She smiled stiffly at him and continued on.

The group at the table ceased their discussion.

Something seemed to prick at Valerie's back. Undoubtedly, it was the looks of several people.

She poured coffee and added sweetener and milk. Turning, she forced her voice to sound cheery. "Good morning."

The group began to talk again. Most of them were older teachers who she didn't know well, but as she placed her mug on the table, Shanna entered the room, and sent her a smile.

Valerie pulled out a chair and Shanna joined her. The art teacher, Paula, looked up from a catalog she was studying and gave Valerie a searching look, before dropping her gaze.

"People are talking about you and Douglas," Shanna said, her voice pitched so low Valerie barely heard her.

Surprised, Valerie stared. "What do you mean?" she whispered back.

"I mean," Shanna whispered, "that someone in the office said that you were at the diner with him and his family."

Valerie started, and her coffee mug clanged against the table, some of it sloshing out of her mug. Luckily the noise level was high and no one except Shanna seemed to notice. She took her napkin and hastily wiped the spill, then brought the mug to her lips.

"Word certainly does get around," Valerie said, not hiding the tart note in her voice. "I can't imagine who saw me. I looked around there and didn't see anyone from the school."

"The school nurse from the high school saw you,"

Shanna continued in a low voice. "She's lived here in Green Valley for ages, I've heard, and probably knows Douglas."

Valerie couldn't recall ever meeting the woman. "I don't know her," she said softly to her friend. "But I have heard that she likes to gossip."

She stopped, hearing the word "traitor" in a loud voice from the end of the table.

Her stomach clenched, and her fingers tightened on the mug. She turned in her seat to look at the group at the end of the table. Sam had been regarding her, but now he averted his eyes.

What a coward, she thought. He can't even accuse me to my face. Not that she deserved the accusation. Valerie was about to say something when Anne breezed into the room.

She looked happy. She'd seen Tony at some point during the weekend, Valerie knew, and they were getting along well. Frankly, she couldn't help being relieved at Anne's entrance. Some of the tension in the room dissipated.

Anne took some coffee and then plopped down in the seat on Valerie's other side. "How's everything?"

"Fine," Valerie said, raising her voice and looking straight at Sam.

He muttered something to the teacher next to him, and bent over his lesson plan book.

Anne pitched her voice low. "The word is out about you seeing Douglas again. I heard the secretaries in the main office talking about it when I came in."

"I might as well announce it on the radio," Valerie grumbled.

Shanna piped up. "You haven't done anything wrong. If Mr. Handsome-Board-Member asked me out, I'd go in a minute."

Valerie had to laugh. "Thanks." Still, although she wasn't ashamed, she was uncomfortable. And she was beginning to feel like she was being watched through binoculars. The worst thing she could do, she decided, was to act embarrassed. That would make the cynics like Sam think she really was hiding something.

Five teachers entered the staff room, one right behind the other. Although Ruby gave Valerie a wide smile and a wink, two teachers behind her stared balefully at Valerie.

She met their looks head-on. But she was feeling more and more uneasy. There was definite tension in the room. She tried to ignore it, chatting with her friends. Ruby and Anne were enthusiastic about their dates this past weekend, and Shanna lamented the fact that she hadn't been meeting any guys lately.

The warning bell rang, signaling it was time for teachers to get to their classrooms and hall posts. Valerie held her head high as she left the room, conscious of a few more looks.

She was actually in a good position, she told herself. She had nothing to hide—because everyone already knew she was seeing Douglas.

There were, however, some unexpected reactions.

That afternoon, the negotiations team held a meeting in Bernie's classroom at the high school. The minute she and Anne walked in, Al came up to Valerie.

"Is it true you're dating Douglas Cooper?" he demanded, a wary look on his face.

Word sure gets around, Valerie thought. She wondered briefly if there was an underground spy network in town. "We've gone out a few times," Valerie said, trying to keep her voice neutral.

The teachers who were already there turned to regard her. "Hey, that might be good," Phyllis said. "Maybe he'll start to see things from our viewpoint."

Al was shaking his head. "That's doubtful." He turned to look at Bernie. "Is that a conflict of interest, do you think?"

Bernie sent Valerie a kind look. "Actually, it might not

be a bad thing," he stated. "It might make him more agreeable to our demands."

"It's not like it's never occurred here before," Phyllis added.

"Really?" Anne asked, with great interest.

"Sure. In the last twenty years, we've had two teachers married to board members."

Anne shot Valerie a look. "Who was that?" she continued, as they drew up chairs.

"Edna Schmidt—the English teacher who retired three years ago—her husband was on the Board for years. And then there was Maryann Terelli—she taught at Lincoln Elementary before you started here, Valerie—her husband was a teacher in Sussex County, and he was on the board here for a couple of terms."

That was news to Valerie, and Anne, but Bernie and the others were nodding. They seemed to know the individuals Phyllis was talking about.

And something inside Valerie was cheering at Phyllis' words.

She tried to push thoughts of board members married to teachers aside as they got down to brainstorming. But the thoughts came pulsating through her mind; if those people could work around the situation, why couldn't she and Douglas?

Douglas called that evening and left a message while Valerie was at an aerobics class with Shanna. When she returned his call, she got his sister-in-law, Jessica, who was watching the kids because Douglas was at a meeting.

She went to sleep early, which was a good thing, she decided the following day.

Her class, which was usually pretty good except for Scarlett and Dustin, was acting up. Badly. And it was requiring every shred of patience for Valerie to deal with them.

Scarlett had been more subdued for almost a week—

maybe her mother had spoken to her, Valerie had thought hopefully. But today she'd started picking on Kayla and had the other girl in tears twice. Valerie spoke to Scarlett, sternly, but thought it wasn't helping much, and was considering making her stay after school the following day and letting Scarlett's mother know.

Before she could give it much thought, she had to get the next reading group together, and then a ruckus broke out at the back of the room. This time, it was Dustin and Jason. As Valerie rushed over, Scarlett sidled into the fight and was soon supporting Jason. Jorge and a girl named Amanda stood up for Dustin, and Valerie had to break up the verbal skirmish and order everyone back to their seats, with threats of staying after school and loss of privileges.

She was glad when lunch time finally arrived.

"Is it a full moon?" she asked Ruby.

"I'll have to check the calendar. My class is acting up too," Ruby replied.

"Mine too," Shanna said, seating herself next to Ruby. "Maybe it's the weather. We've got a storm coming."

Valerie glanced out the window. Slate-gray clouds skidded across the sky. They were beautiful in a stark way, and heralded rain.

After lunch, Valerie's class seemed even more tense. It became apparent that the class was becoming divided and taking sides.

Perturbed, Valerie managed to be strict with the students and keep a lid on the problem. But she was afraid it might get worse. By the time school ended, she had a headache, which was unusual for her.

She sat in her room after the students left, and tried to finish correcting papers. Finally, she decided to go home, get comfortable, and finish there.

She was home less than an hour when Douglas called.

"Hi," he said, and her heart jumped when she heard his voice.

"Hi," she said, scooting down on the couch with the

cordless phone to her ear. Cleo, ensconced in the large chair, stared at her accusingly. On gray days like this, the cats liked to sleep a lot, and the phone had woken Cleo up. King was curled on the other end of the couch. He hadn't moved when it rang.

She spoke with Douglas for a few minutes, mostly about Lindsay and Matt. Then Douglas asked if she wanted to go to the movies on Saturday night.

"I can't," she said regretfully. She would like to be with him—although she knew it might be best if they had some space from each other. Because although she loved him, she didn't know if what he felt for her was genuine caring—or just a desire to complete his family and get a mom for his niece and nephew.

"I'm going to see my mom on Saturday," she continued. "I'm picking up my heavy winter coats which I have stored at her house—I don't have much closet space here—and having dinner with her and my aunt."

They spoke for a few more minutes, then Douglas had to get off the phone and take Lindsay to her dance class.

Valerie sat back with a sigh. She wanted to see him.

But was that a good idea? She'd had no indication from Douglas that he felt anything more than a strong interest in her. Sure, he liked to kiss her but that didn't mean he was in love.

What if she ended up with a broken heart, like she had with Stuart? And this time it would be much worse. Because what she felt for Douglas was much, much stronger than anything she'd ever felt for Stuart.

As soon as they'd cleaned up the hamburger casserole he'd made for dinner, and fed and walked the dog, Douglas made sure his nephew and niece were finishing their homework. Then he went into his study to call Valerie again. "How about if we get together on Friday?" he said without preamble.

"Friday?" She paused. "Douglas, I'm not sure . . . that is,

part of me would like to see you, but . . ." her voice trailed off.

"But?" He frowned. But what?"

She was sounding strangely hesitant. Which wasn't really like the vibrant woman he knew. He waited, and she added, "My seeing you is causing some controversy at school."

"Yeah? People have said stuff to me too," he said. "I just ignore them."

"They have?" She sounded astonished.

"Yeah. Carl Warren even—" He stopped. "Well," he began, figuring he should be honest with her, "he hinted that I should be trying to pry information out of you."

"What!? That's terrible." Now she sounded indignant.

"I told him to forget it. And I suggest you tell anyone who gives you a hard time the same." He leaned back in his chair.

She laughed, but the sound wasn't humor-filled. "It's a little more difficult for me. You're in kind of an administrative position. People won't be as hard on you. I have a lot of colleagues I see daily, and—well, there's more pressure."

"Ignore them," he repeated.

Silence.

Then, she said, "I'll try." She sounded more decisive this time.

"So, what about Friday?" he pressed.

"Okay," she agreed. There was a moment's hesitiaton, and then she asked, "Why don't you come here? I'll make dinner."

A homemade meal? That he didn't cook? With Valerie! His mouth was watering already. "That would be super!" he declared.

They spoke for a few minutes. Then Valerie told him she had a ton of papers to finish correcting.

"Okay," he said. She seemed anxious to get off the phone, and he wondered why. Why, when she had seemed so content in his arms just a few days before. He'd thought they were getting closer. Was he wrong? He said goodbye, and slowly replaced the phone.

Why was she hesitant about getting together this weekend? Was she really going to see her mother, or was there something else going on?

Or *someone* else?

He frowned. Someone else? Could Valerie be seeing someone besides him?

He clenched his hands. He didn't like the thought. Not at all.

The photo he'd taken of Valerie the day they'd gone pumpkin-picking sat on his desk. He'd printed it out from the computer, and now he lifted and studied it.

She looked beautiful and happy. She'd been smiling at him when he took the photo. The thought of her smiling for someone else twisted his insides.

Chapter Eleven

Music sounded softly through the door to Valerie's apartment as Douglas climbed the last set of steps. He wondered how good a cook Valerie was. He'd been looking forward to this dinner with great anticipation. A home cooked meal with a woman he liked—a lot—what could be better? It wasn't until now that it had occurred to him to wonder how talented she was in the kitchen. He wasn't a bad cook himself, although his repertoire of dishes was limited. Maybe, he thought hopefully, Valerie was as good at cooking as she was at teaching.

He rapped on the door to Valerie's apartment, shifting his weight. "Hi!" he called.

"Hi!" she answered, and opened the door.

Delectable smells pounced on him immediately.

Even in jeans and a simple red sweater, she looked lovely. He bent to give her a quick kiss, brushing her soft lips with his own, then going back to linger for a long moment. Did he imagine she sighed with pleasure? Then she stepped back.

He handed her the autumn bouquet he'd picked up.

"Flowers? How sweet!" she exclaimed. "Thank you."

The spicy aroma from the kitchen was making his mouth water. "Something smells wonderful," he said eagerly.

"It's almost ready," she said.

He followed her through the bedroom into the kitchen, where the table was set and simple white candles stood in cut glass candle holders. She filled a vase with water and set the flowers on the table, slightly to the side. The two cats were perched on some kind of carpeted cat tower, with places for them to lay and stare at him. He smiled and said, "Hi cats." One blinked, and the other yawned.

"Need any help?" he asked.

"No, everything's done," she told him. She lit the candles, and gave him a salad to toss.

They spoke about Matthew and Lindsay, and Valerie told him a little about some of her students. Douglas described some funny customers he'd had this week as they started on salad and home-made garlic bread.

"This is even better than what we had in the restaurant," he observed, taking a second slice. If the bread was any indication, he was in for a wonderful meal.

The main course was home made lasagna, and was absolutely delicious.

Valerie would make the perfect wife.

The thought popped into his mind like a bombshell.

He ate with enthusiasm, complimenting her liberally on the meal as they talked about their families. He tried not to spend much time contemplating that last revelation that had bombarded his consciousness. He'd do that later.

"Thanks," she said. "Really, it's not that hard—it just takes some time."

"No, believe me, no one's ever made me such a good meal," he told her. He covered her small hand with his own. Her skin was smooth and soft, and he caressed her hand slowly.

They regarded each other quietly for a moment, and he wondered what she was thinking. Then she squeezed his hand and withdrew hers, returning to the meal.

He helped her clean up, and she suggested they have dessert a little later. He agreed readily, and they took coffee into the living room, where Valerie put on a jazz CD.

Now he could look forward to something else delicious— the feel of Valerie. The minute she put her coffee down on a table, he drew her into his arms.

"I've missed you," he said huskily, and kissed her.

Her arms wound around his neck and she kissed him back, murmuring softly.

Kissing Valerie was nothing like kissing any other woman. She was sweeter than wine, and holding her was absolutely wonderful. He would be perfectly happy savoring the feel of her in his arms for hours . . . days . . . weeks . . .

The heady sensations spinning through his entire being were like nothing he'd ever experienced before. He felt terrific. Better than terrific. He felt like he must be glowing.

They kissed and kissed, and Douglas was conscious of the desire to have the evening go on without end. But after a while, Valerie extricated herself from his hold. "We should have dessert," she said, and he caught a note of reluctance—or caution—in her tone.

He shook his head, trying to clear it of the overwhelming feelings that kissing Valerie caused. "And I can't stay late," he said, regretfully. "The girl next door is watching the kids but she's not allowed to stay out too late. She's only thirteen."

They ate the white cake with chocolate icing Valerie had baked, and it was as delicious as dinner. She insisted on giving him a generous portion to take home for his niece and nephew.

"Are you really seeing your mother tomorrow?" he asked abruptly.

"Yes, and my aunt." She looked surprised, and paused in the act of covering the paper plate holding the cake with Saran wrap. "Why do you ask?"

"Oh, nothing." he said lightly. But when he went to leave, he wrapped Valerie in his arms and kissed her intensely. If she was going to see someone else—a male someone else—he was going to make sure he gave her something to remember.

* * *

"So how are the negotiations going?"

Valerie eyed her mother, who was perched on her old bed in the room she used to share with Jillian. Louise McFadden was an attractive woman who looked young for her age, despite losing her husband a few years ago.

"Not so well," she admitted, as she pulled her good winter coat and a heavy, more casual jacket from the closet. Both were wrapped in plastic from the dry cleaners and slid in her arms. She deposited them on her sister's bed, then reached in for a couple of sweatshirts she'd left at home too. "I wish I had more closet space."

"Well, you have more room in your apartment than Jillian does, what with her sharing with the other three girls," her mother pointed out.

"I know, but Jillian's is temporary. She'll be out of law school in another year." Valerie lifted the summer dresses and some pants she'd brought from her apartment to store here for the winter, and placed them in the closet where the coats had hung.

"Why aren't the negotiations going well?" her mother asked.

Valerie straightened the clothes in the closet, including a few things she always left there in case she unexpectedly stayed over. She stepped back into the room, and briefly, she described the meetings they'd held so far and the board's unwillingness to move. She left out any mention of Douglas.

She'd barely been able to think of anything else *but* Douglas. Last night she had felt totally in love, enveloped in his embrace, reveling in the magic of his kisses. Like nothing in the world could come between them. But in the morning, she once again had doubts.

"Hmm, it doesn't sound as if your side is moving much either," her mother remarked.

"That's not true," Valerie protested. "We've made some concessions."

"But not too many."

"Well, we can't make too many. We need room to maneuver," Valerie pointed out. "It's like a game—a bargaining game."

"I know. Your father's friend Raymond was on the negotiations team for years, remember? It sounds like the board is playing by the same rules you are."

Was the board playing by the same rules the teachers were? Valerie wondered.

"They did give in on the grandparents' bereavement day," her mother continued.

Valerie shrugged. "It makes sense."

"You seem especially intense about it," her mother said, looking at Valerie carefully.

Valerie wondered if her mom knew there was more to the story than just negotiations. She sat back down on her sister's bed, smoothing a dark red sweatshirt. "It's because of Dad," she said. "I feel very strongly that I have to try to improve the lot of my fellow teachers. They don't get paid enough. Look at Dad—working all those extra jobs, all those hours, pushing himself into an early grave because his job didn't pay enough."

Louise McFadden straightened her back. "It's true that when he was first teaching the pay was poor," she said. "But it did improve as you kids got older. And no one said he had to work all those jobs."

"I didn't mean that you pushed him into it,' Valerie said. "I know you didn't. Dad was driven by himself." It was true, she knew. Her mother hadn't been the kind to nag her husband to earn more money. "It's just that we needed the money."

"Needed it? Not exactly, honey. Your father wanted it," her mother said.

"But it costs a lot of money to raise kids, and he always said they didn't pay teachers enough."

"That's true," her mother said. "But after you kids were all in school, I went back to work at the bank. And we were doing alright. By then your father's parents had passed away, and left us some money too. But Johnny was still driven to make extra money. Don't you realize why?"

"What are you talking about?" Valerie asked, frowning.

"You know our story. My parents had more money than your father's family. They felt he was a 'poor boy' going into a profession where he'd make very little."

"Yes, I remember you telling us that a long time ago," Valerie said. She sat back further.

"They didn't want me to marry him. But I loved your father and he loved me. And he swore he'd take good care of me and provide for our family well."

Valerie stared, listening to her mother.

"So early on he got his Master's degree and took on other jobs. He was determined to prove he could support us all in style, the style your grandparents expected."

Shock bounced through Valerie. "He was trying to prove to Grandma and Grandpa that he could provide for us?" She gripped the folds of the sweatshirt.

"Yes," her mother said, and sighed. "Of course, your father was the type who did like to keep busy—like your sister and brother—but if he wasn't taking extra jobs, he could have played recreational sports or something else. When we were first dating, he was really into bowling. I wish he had continued with it—he used to enjoy it so much." She sighed again.

"I always thought he just didn't make enough money," Valerie said.

"Well, we wouldn't have lived quite so well, but we would have done okay. He made more than a lot of other people."

"But I heard him talk about how teachers were underpaid and undervalued, many times," Valerie stated. "And how he only planned to have two children, because of the cost—but then the twins came along—"

"That's true. He did fervently believe teachers were underpaid," her mother said. "And he loved teaching, like you do, and felt it was an important calling. He also felt sorry for those who were struggling. But *we* weren't."

Tears crept into Valerie's eyes. "I'm sorry, Mom," she said. "All that work, for nothing."

"Don't be sorry, dear," her mother said. "Johnny lived life fully, the way he wished. He chose this way to live. Of course I miss him—but he did have a happy life. most of all, he got pleasure from watching his kids grow up into fine people. And he was thrilled that he had three. I actually think he secretly wanted more than two anyway."

Louise stood up. Valerie caught a trace of tears in her mother's eyes. "Now then, I hear the dryer buzzer. I'll go and see if your jeans are dry."

Valerie stared at the door for several minutes after her mother left the room.

She had heard the stories about her maternal grandparents frowning on her parents' marriage. How they thought Johnny wasn't "good enough." They had died when Valerie was still young, so she didn't remember them clearly. But she hadn't connected those facts to the reason that her father was driven to work so hard. Not that it changed her own feelings about negotiations. She was still committed to helping her fellow teachers. But it did give her another perspective on her father's life. Perhaps Douglas had been correct when he suggested her father could be a workaholic.

She'd have to give this revelation more thought, when she was alone.

She got up, and went down to help with the loads of laundry she'd brought home. Going to the laundromat and then dragging her things up several flight of stairs was a chore, and whenever she came home, she'd bring at least a couple of loads of wash with her.

She found her mother folding jeans.

"I'll do that," she said, taking the pile from her mom.

Her mother's cat, Molly, a tiger stripe, was weaving in and out between her legs. She was older than Cleo and

King, nearly ten, and didn't want to play the way they did. Valerie bent down and scratched her.

She'd brought her cats down for the weekend, and now King strolled into the laundry room, followed by her mother's dog, Laddie, a Sheltie. "Have you been getting out much?" she asked her mom.

"Yes. Especially with your Aunt Jean." Her mother's older sister had been widowed only a year after Valerie's dad had died. "She's trying to fix me up with one of her neighbors. She's dating a friend of his."

"Well, you should go," Valerie urged. "If you don't like him, you don't have to date him again."

"Maybe." Her mother turned to scrutinize Valerie. "And what about you? Are you seeing anyone?"

"Well . . ." Valerie hesitated, then mentioned her dates with Douglas. She tried to keep it casual. She hadn't admitted to anyone that she loved Douglas. The feeling was too new to talk about yet.

"If you really like him, I'd go out with him some more," her mother said. "And see what happens. Don't let the fact that he's on the board stop you. His niece and nephew are nice kids?"

"Oh, yes," Valerie said.

Her mother frowned suddenly. "Believe it or not," she said, "your old boyfriend Stuart called. He was looking for you."

"He called me at home too," Valerie admitted.

"I think he wants to see you again." Her mother shook her head. "I wouldn't give him your phone number, but he knew from some of your old friends you were living out in Warren County."

"My number's listed. He probably called information or looked on the Internet," Valerie said. So Stuart had called a few of her friends. No wonder he'd learned what area she lived in. There must be hundreds of McFaddens in New Jersey, but he'd managed to find her. "Don't worry, I'm not going to waste time with Stuart," she said firmly. As she said the words, she knew how true they were.

She switched the topic and they chatted about her class, then got ready to do some shopping. After an hour spent at a large discount shoe store, they both splurged on two pairs of shoes, and met her aunt at the restaurant for an early dinner.

They were home by seven thirty. They watched television for a while, but by nine-thirty her mother was yawning, and went to bed. Both Louise McFadden and Valerie's brother Jared were morning people. Valerie, her sister Jillian and Johnny had always been the night people in the family.

Valerie watched some more television. Then she let the dog out for his last run, saw him settle down to sleep in her mom's room, and wandered upstairs.

All three cats were sprawled in corners of the bedroom she'd shared with Jill. She got ready for bed and curled up with the romance she was reading, and when she got tired, she turned off the light. Closing her eyes, she couldn't help reliving the passionate kisses she'd shared with Douglas the day before.

Sunday night Valerie had a brief conversation with Douglas on the phone, and promised to see him later in the week. She still had conflicting feelings about him. She wanted to see him badly—but would it only hurt her in the end?

She spent time thinking about the growing animosity in her class. Most of the kids were good kids, they were just having a problem and a couple of the students were egging the others on. She wondered how her father would have handled it—except that he had older students, of course. He, she was sure, would have been able to talk them into getting along better.

Monday morning her class behaved fairly well. But after they returned from lunch, the kids seemed to have formed into two camps again, and there were rumblings and dirty looks among them. Valerie started teaching a science lesson, and halfway through Dustin suddenly yelled out, "He took my pen!" He glared at Jason.

"Did not!" Jason declared.

"I saw him, he didn't—" Scarlett interrupted.

"Did too—"

Jason muttered something.

A couple of kids gasped, and Valerie knew it must have been an offensive word.

Dustin stood up, his fists clenched.

"That's it," Valerie said firmly, gripping the chalk in her hand so hard it broke in two. "We are going to talk about this situation right now. And we are going to work to solve this problem. I don't want this getting out of hand and spoiling Halloween." She was smart enough not to threaten anything she couldn't carry through on, but she was aware that the implied threat would get the students' attention.

Temporarily putting aside the lesson on the moon, she moved closer to her class, hands on hips. "Everyone sit down." Her voice was commanding, and her tone had all the students paying attention. Her brain raced ahead, forging a plan.

She reached for another piece of chalk, and began writing on the chalkboard, *"Rules of Our Class."*

"We did this the first day of school," one of the girls pointed out.

"That's right," Valerie said. She forced herself not to sound too angry. A reasonable but firm tone would do more for the kids than pure anger. "Now, I'm going to divide you up." She then divided the class by seats, not by the factions they had placed themselves in.

"Things have been getting bad lately," she began. "Now, I know that you are all good kids. But we are having a problem and I want it to stop this instant. I do not want to start calling parents and the principal. I want to try to solve this ourselves." She picked up papers and began passing them out. "I want you to take a few minutes and brain-storm. Make up a list of rules that you think the other group should follow. You can refer to our class rules if you want, and you may talk as long as you talk quietly."

The groups began working at once, whispering, occasionally giggling, and sometimes sending the other group a speculative glance. Valerie wrote down the names of students in each group. She had had another idea she thought the students would like, and she could use it as a little bribery. After ten minutes she stopped them. "That's enough to start," she said. She called on Amanda to read her group's rules.

The list was logical. The other group should be polite and respect all the students; there was to be no stealing, name-calling, cheating or physical acts of any kind. Then Valerie called on Jorge, who ran down a list that was almost identical.

"These are all very good rules," Valerie said at the conclusion. "Especially about respecting other people, and ourselves. Now, do you all think you can abide by these rules?"

Every head nodded, and a few students said, "Yes."

"I'm going to hold you to that," Valerie said. "Now, I will give you some liberties. If this doesn't work, we will go back to this seating arrangement. But I will let you try picking your own seats, and we'll see if you can manage to behave and then you can keep these seats."

There were gasps of pleasure.

"Spend a few minutes picking your seats, and when we're done, then we'll move the contents of your desks."

Within five minutes, while Valerie thought rapidly, the students sorted themselves out, with a minimum of whispered bickering. Valerie noted that Dustin and Jason were far apart. Kayla was sitting near Amanda and Lisa, both good students, and Scarlett had arrayed herself with a couple of other nice girls like Cassandra.

"Do you think you can abide by these rules?" Valerie had written most of them on the board.

The class chorused, "Yes."

One boy raised his hand. "What if some of them don't?" he challenged.

Valerie turned and wrote on the board, COMPROMISE, in upper-case letters. Turning back to the class, she said, "See this word? Compromise. It means everyone is going to have to make some adjustments—some give and take. One day you may get your way, the next day your friend will. Or you may end up meeting in the middle on some issues. It means no one is going to get their way *all* the time."

As Valerie talked, it was as if half of her brain had split off, whirling away on a separate path, following its own direction. *Compromise*. Give and take. Here she was telling her students to compromise, to be fair—when she hadn't exactly been doing the same. The negotiations team should be practicing the same principles as her pupils. No one side was going to get its way on everything. The teachers were no different than the students in her class.

Wasn't that what the whole process was about? Give and take? In her enthusiasm, her desire to make things better for her colleagues, she had forgotten that. And so, she suspected, had all the members of the negotiating teams.

She kept speaking to her students, and when she felt they truly understood the idea of compromise, gave them a break for a few minutes. Then they took some time to change the contents of their desks to their new seats, and Valerie suggested cleaning out their desks to start fresh. By the time they were done, school was close to ending. Rather than try to start the science lesson again, she asked them to write in their journals and planned to rearrange her schedule so they could fit in the remainder of the lesson.

At dismissal, Valerie reminded them of their homework assignments and then stood by the door as the first group of buses was called. She couldn't wait to jot down some of her new ideas for negotiations.

"Goodbye!" she said.

"Bye! Bye Miss McFadden," they said, and left the room, chattering.

They already looked and sounded more positive, Valerie thought. She determined to bring in the spooky stories and start reading them tomorrow, although she'd originally planned to wait a few more days. She hoped the positive reinforcement would help.

The kids who walked home were called, and then only the ones on the second group of buses remained. When they were called, she immediately sat down and began to write.

Once she'd written down the basics of her ideas, she sped through correcting the papers she had piled up on her desk. When she completed the papers, she closed up her room, glad no one had come by to talk or interrupt her work.

Valerie's thoughts were crystal-clear. Neither side would get everything they wanted. Their goal was something fair they could all live with. She'd forgotten to look at the big picture, obsessing over the details. Compromise was the key. Both in her classroom and at the negotiations table.

Not that she would give up her ideals—or those of her father. No, change would come gradually. The teachers couldn't get everything they wanted. And neither could the board of education.

She strode to her car, her step determined.

Once home, she changed, spent some time with King and Cleo, who were still tired from the weekend trip, and then sat down at her computer.

She worked quickly, typing in the ideas she'd started in school, then developing them. Eventually the cats began making noise and she realized it was after six o'clock and dinner time. She fed them, had soup and a sandwich, and then finished her work.

She was pleased with what she had accomplished. She

had come up with what she thought was a good proposal for the board, and wanted to discuss it with the team the following day.

When she came out of the shower she saw her answering machine blinking. The call had been from Douglas. But by that time it was well after nine, and she felt drained. She decided to call him tomorrow, and crawling into bed, she felt better than she had the last few nights. Quickly, she went to sleep.

Valerie's class was calmer the following day. After a speedy review of the rules they'd generated the day before and a couple of additional suggestions from her class rules from the beginning of the year, they got down to work. She was impressed by the new mood of cooperation among them, and pride in working for the student-generated regulations. Even Scarlett seemed nicer.

At lunchtime, Valerie confided her plan to Anne, who was encouraging. Valerie called Bernie and asked him if the team could meet a little earlier this evening so she could go over her idea.

The afternoon continued to be a pleasant one. Valerie was able to squeeze in the science lesson and then had time for two spooky stories. The class sat, enthralled, and begged for more. "If you continue to do so well, I'll read a couple more tomorrow," she promised.

She had errands to do after school. She ate an early dinner and then dressed in her favorite red suit. By six-thirty she was at the high school, and the members of the teachers' team began straggling in. This time Donna, their union president, had come too.

Bernie told the others that Valerie had a special idea and indicated she should speak.

"There's something I've been working on," Valerie started.

The others listened expectantly.

"We're in this to get the best deal we can for our fellow

teachers," she stated. "But we must not lose sight of the fact that the whole negotiations process is one of *compromise*. Neither side will get everything it wants. Our goal is a fair contract, something we can live with, with some gains over the previous contract."

Bernie nodded slightly, and Phyllis looked thoughtful.

She plunged ahead. "With that in mind, I propose we tell the board what I've just said. We should then suggest that to save money—and time—we should stop beating around the bush and get straight down to serious talking. We should drop the most ridiculous of our demands, and so should they. I'd like to suggest that they drop the idea of our paying our own insurance costs right now. In return, we'll drop the demand for the 19% pay raise and go to 7% or 7.5% for each year the next two years. And we'll drop our demand for an expanded prescription plan. I just don't see it in the cards for this year if we want the money."

Valerie went on to describe the situation in her class, and how the spirit of compromise was working out.

"So," she finished, "what do all of you think?"

"I think it's a good idea," Phyllis declared. "We waste so much time each year with this game-playing."

"How do we know they'll be as realistic as we will be?" Al demanded.

"There're no guarantees," Valerie admitted. "I think we have to have some trust here. I think we should show we're bargaining in good faith."

"Are you sure there's no other motives?" Al continued.

Valerie looked him straight in the eyes. "If you're referring to the fact that I've gone out a few times with Douglas Cooper, no, I don't have other motives."

"I think it's worth trying," Bernie said. "That's the way it was in the old days—I'm talking forty years ago when I started teaching. Negotiations didn't get as stretched out. Frankly, I think this game-playing is a waste of everyone's valuable time."

"I agree," Anne said staunchly. "The only one who benefits from a long, drawn out negotiations process is the board lawyer!"

"But what if the board isn't willing to meet us halfway?" Jim asked.

"I think if they hear Valerie talk, they'll give it a try," Donna said. "She convinced me!"

Valerie had hoped they'd want her to speak. "If it doesn't work," she said, "we can always go back to our usual methods."

Bernie stood up, placing his hands on the table, and smiled. "I think we have a good shot at this. Let's do it!"

Chapter Twelve

"To start, we have a team member who has some sug-gestions for our negotiations process," Bernie said, looking in turn at each one of the board members. "I'd like to turn the meeting over to Valerie McFadden."

Douglas sat up straighter. Since he entered the room, he'd barely been able to keep his eyes off Valerie. As usual, she looked gorgeous. But today she wore a very serious expression, and he'd wondered what was up.

Now he had every reason in the world to watch her and listen carefully.

She stood and went to stand by Bernie's seat. The older man gave her a swift smile before gesturing her to go ahead. She began by talking about a situation in her class-room, where students became divided and soon there was an atmosphere of distrust and strife.

Then she discussed how she'd gotten the students to make up rules and to try to compromise. "I realized that many of these same principles could be applied to the ne-gotiations process," she continued. "We teachers want the best contracts we can get for our members. You board members, of course, want what you feel is in the best in-terest of the citizens of Green Valley." She paused, and shifted to place hands on the back of Bernie's and Phyllis' chairs. "We must remember," she said, her voice rising, "that the whole negotiations process is one of compromise. Neither side will get everything it wants. Our goal is a fair contract, something we can both live with." Her gaze moved from one board member to the next.

Douglas thought her eyes lingered on him a shade longer than on anyone else. Or had he imagined it? But he didn't imagine the warmth that shot through him at her gaze, nor the heightened awareness that switched on in him from the moment she'd started her impassioned speech: "Compromise, ladies and gentlemen, is the key. If we want to move successfully through life, we must learn how to compromise. It means respecting others and learning to live and work together in a variety of situations. Whether it's with coworkers, siblings, friends, spouses—we all must learn the art of compromise. Otherwise, personal and professional relationships break down. And I believe it is an intrinsic part of the negotiations process.

"With this in mind," she said, switching her position slightly, "I want to propose eliminating some of the game-playing that often, sadly, goes on at these meetings. Instead, let's get straight to the heart of a fair settlement. Everyone is pressed for time; if we can get right down to serious business, we can shorten the whole process and arrive at a fair settlement."

She turned to look at Bernie. "Will you outline our ideas?"

Bernie took over, and Douglas watched as Valerie moved back to her seat. He guessed she had carefully rehearsed her speech, and he agreed whole heartedly with everything she'd said. He wanted to cheer. And he found himself enormously proud of the way she'd handled the speech.

The other teachers were sending her smiles and nods. Douglas had the urge to jump up and kiss her, and had to tamp down the impulse. But when she met his eyes a moment later, he winked and smiled.

Bernie was outlining the teacher's new proposal, which was not even in written form yet. Douglas listened carefully and jotted some notes. A 7.5% raise this next year and 7%

even the next. They would drop their demand for expanded pharmaceutical coverage if the board would drop the idea of having the teachers pay for their insurance.

Mr. Tyler suggested a caucus, and the board went back to the board office, convening in the main room there.

"It's about time we got straight down to business," Carl Warren said firmly. He shot Douglas a look. "Son, that little lady has a good head on her shoulders."

And a warm heart, Douglas thought, but didn't say it aloud.

"I think it's a good idea." The usually quiet Mrs. Zinkowski spoke up. "We had talked amongst ourselves about giving the teachers five to seven percent raises. Let's split it and suggest six percent this year."

"I don't know," Marvin Tyler said slowly. "If we give in too fast, they may ask for more. Give 'em an inch, they'll take a mile."

Anger rushed through Douglas. "But from everything you guys have told me, the old way of negotiating wastes a lot of time—and we usually end at the same place we figured we would in the beginning. Let's give this a chance." He voice was firm. He crossed his arms and looked straight at Marvin Tyler. The others were slowly nodding their heads. Even the board lawyer didn't look negative.

"It could shorten the process considerably if you got to the gist of things," Mr. Moore said.

Maybe he, too, was tired of the late nights, Douglas thought.

With everyone else in agreement, the pressure was on Marvin Tyler to capitulate. He complained but when Douglas pointed out to him that a reasonable settlement, made quickly, would help with Tyler's own re-election in the spring, he grumbled and gave in.

"Alright, we'll try it your way," he said to Douglas. "But I won't be responsible if the teachers suddenly go back on their word."

"They won't." Douglas was absolutely positive of that fact.

He heard Marvin Tyler mutter something about ulterior motives under his breath, but decided that, since he was giving in, it would be best to ignore the man's comment. After a short discussion, they returned to the conference room, where Carl Warren took the lead this time.

Douglas searched for Valerie and when his eyes met hers, gave her another quick wink.

"In the interest of expediting the negotiations process," Carl said, "we agree with your team's views. We will drop our—suggestion—that the teachers pay for their own health insurance if the teachers agree to waive the demand for the expanded prescription plan. We are offering a raise of 6%."

Douglas could tell from a couple of quick smiles that they were in the ballpark now and the teachers were pleased. Bernie said that all the suggestions would be put in writing and that they would meet in a few weeks to refine the agreements made tonight. Mrs. Haggerty, who had remained silent all evening, clicked quickly on her laptop and then looked up with a satisfied smile.

Douglas felt near-triumph, and knew it wasn't just because it looked like the negotiations were going to be settled more easily this year than in the past. He felt triumphant for Valerie. Her plan had succeeded! He had to fight to keep himself from bursting into applause. Instead, he simply smiled at her.

She gave him a quick smile back, then turned to Bernie, who was speaking. He was expressing, in rather formal terms, the teachers' appreciation for the board's cooperation and assured the board members that the teachers would continue to be flexible so that negotiations could be concluded in the near future.

Bernie and Marvin Tyler shook hands, and when the teachers left, several of them wore smiles.

Valerie sent Douglas another glance and then she, too, left.

Back in the faculty room, the teachers congratulated each other, and the mood was almost festive. Valerie sagged into the old couch, both happy and relieved.

Someone said something about the association hosting another happy hour, and she heard Al caution them to wait a few weeks and make sure the board followed up on their promises. But deep down, she was certain they would.

"It looks like, for the first time in more than a couple of decades, we'll be able to wrap up negotiations quickly," Bernie said. He smiled at Valerie. "Thank you for everything you've done."

"I didn't do it alone," Valerie said, smiling back. "You all helped—especially you, Bernie."

The thought lingered in her mind that Douglas had helped too. Instinct told her that he had persuaded the other board members that hers was a good idea. And although there would be some more smoothing out to do, she had no doubt it could be accomplished with a minimum of controversy.

The teachers left the building, joking and laughing, with smiles on their faces. Valerie noticed that even the normally worried-looking Al looked positive.

When she arrived home, Valerie walked up the stairs slowly, feeling happy but drained. It had been a long day. A very long day. She was yawning by the time she got to her door.

She pulled on her pajamas, spent some time with the cats, and then tumbled into bed.

The phone rang, but she was too weary to pick it up. And it was late. She listened for the answering machine to click on, in case it was urgent. But whoever it was left no message.

Was it silly to hope it had been Douglas?

                              *   *   *

Wednesday was a clear and bright day, and the mood of the class matched the weather. Valerie was quick to praise her pupils for continuing to behave better and uphold their rules. She smiled when she overheard Scarlett telling Dustin how important it was for the students to get along.

"My mother says in the corporate world," Scarlett stated with great authority, "everyone has to get along to get things done. So we should learn how to do that in school."

Valerie was pleased that Scarlett's mother had apparently decided to talk to her daughter after all. "That's very true," she said to Scarlett and Dustin. "Your mother is right, Scarlett." Scarlett beamed, and Valerie knew that inside was a little girl who did want to please and to get positive attention. She'd been following her mother's poor example of critical remarks. "And you're doing very well," Valerie added with an encouraging smile.

Later that day, when the office called over the public address system asking Valerie to send someone down to pick up some forms, she chose Scarlett for the desired task. Scarlett practically skipped out of the room, her head held high.

With Scarlett behaving better, Kayla and Dustin seemed more confident too.

At dismissal, she let the first group go, then chatted with the others waiting to be called next.

"Hi!" a voice called from the door as the kids who walked were called.

She looked up to see Lindsay smiling at her. Valerie approached her, smiling too. "How are you?" she asked the girl. "Getting ready for Halloween?'

"Yes," she answered. "Val—Miss McFadden," she said, "do your cats like dogs?"

Valerie furrowed her brow. Where had that question come from? "Yes," she said. "They see my mother's dog when I visit there and they get along okay. Why do you ask?"

Lindsay shrugged elaborately. "I just wondered. Riley

likes cats; sometimes our neighbor's cat comes to visit her."
As the next group was called for the buses, she said, "I
gotta go! Bye!" and ran off before Valerie could say anything else.

That was strange, Valerie thought. Animals must be on
her mind.

Dismissal finished and Valerie sat down to work on her
lesson plans. By 3:45 she was ready to leave and locked
her room, humming. She was feeling so good she stopped
at a store on the way home and treated herself to a new
sweater.

She climbed up the steps and let herself into the apartment. The cats picked up on her lively mood and she played
with them for a while, before changing into jeans and a
sweatshirt and making herself coffee. Then she sat down
on the couch to look at her mail. The answering machine
was blinking with two messages. She rewound it, and listened.

"Hey, Val." It was Stuart. "When am I going to hear
from you, babe?"

His voice closely resembled one of her students in whining mode.

Never, Valerie thought.

Even if she still loved him—which she definitely
didn't—she would never marry Stuart just because he'd
had a change of heart. The man was self-centered and used
to doing what he wanted. And she didn't love him.

"Call me soon!" he finished in a commanding tone.

The next call was from Douglas.

"Congratulations!" he exclaimed. "You were fantastic
last night, Valerie. Your speech was compelling. I'm sure
that negotiations will be wrapped up quickly because of
your efforts."

His praise sent pleasure cascading throughout her limbs.

"I'd like to see you again as soon as possible," he continued, his voice dropping to a warm, mellow note. "Can

you come over one night this week? Or I can come over there on Saturday—Sean and Jessica can watch the kids."

She sighed with anticipation.

She picked up the phone to tell him Saturday would be perfect.

Chapter Thirteen

The rest of the week continued to go well, with minor disagreements promptly solved. Of course, with Halloween the following week, the kids were a little hyperactive, but there were no serious problems, and Valerie smiled to herself as she closed up the room Friday afternoon.

When she got home, she called Stuart back to tell him she didn't intend to go out with him. She was relieved to get his voice mail, and left him a message, in an ultra-kind tone, saying she felt they had both moved on and a relationship between them wouldn't work. That would put closure on that! she thought with relief.

Douglas was taking her out Saturday, and she couldn't wait. She baked pumpkin muffins for him and the kids, and then sat down to read and relax for the rest of the evening.

He was right on time. Stepping into her apartment, he grabbed her and hugged her tightly. "That was great!" he said. "You're probably the best spokesperson the teachers have ever had."

She laughed, but shook her head. "Oh, no. Bernie's wonderful. I've learned so much from him."

"Well, I know most of this is your doing," he praised. He was appreciative of the muffins and tucked them into the car.

They went out to dinner at a nice restaurant in the next town. They were both in high spirits, and Valerie concentrated on simply being with the man she loved and enjoying his company. And the dinner was enjoyable. Douglas told amusing stories about Matt and Lindsay, and his own child-hood growing up in town. Valerie related some of her own stories.

She even told him what her mother had told her about her father, and his motives for working so many jobs.

Douglas nodded as he listened, and held her hand as she spoke.

They went back to her apartment and she made them both mugs of cocoa. She was tingling, anticipating some serious cuddling, and wondering if Douglas was going to say anything to indicate he was feeling like she was—that he'd fallen in love too. He was so affectionate, and she hoped with all her heart that her feelings were mutual.

He was wearing a serious expression when she returned to the living room. She placed their mugs on the corner table and sat beside Douglas, her heart hammering.

He picked up her hand and stroked it. "Valerie." His voice was quiet. He met her eyes. "I'm so glad things are working out with the negotiations."

"Me too," she said. His fingers carressed her hand, leaving warmth where he touched.

"But even if there are some snarls, it shouldn't make a difference to us," he said.

Her heart was thumping even harder now.

"I agree," she whispered.

"I mean, now that you know the truth about your dad . . ." His voice dwindled, as if he wasn't too sure of himself.

She stared at him. "What do you mean?"

"Well, now that you know your dad was a workaholic, maybe you won't be so consumed about negotiations and money issues." He regarded her.

"Consumed?" Her voice rose in astonishment. "I'm not consumed. How can you say that?"

"But you were! Not that I blame you—I can see why because of your beliefs—but they were wrong."

Sudden tears stung her eyes. "They were *not* wrong. I

still believe teachers are underpaid—it's just that I realize we have to compromise."

"Of course we have to compromise. But I thought you wouldn't be so—militant—about negotiations, about money." His expression had darkened as she stared at him.

"I'm not militant! And my beliefs aren't wrong," she stated hotly.

He ran his hand through his hair, looking frustrated. "Maybe I'm saying this wrong. It's just you sound a lot like Hillary when you talk about teachers' salaries."

Her stomach seemed to plummet down to her toes. "Hillary? How can you compare me to—to *her*?"

They stared at each other. Valerie bit her lip, fighting both the tears and a growing anger.

"You sound like her right now."

The cold note in his voice shook her.

"I'm not! I—" She stopped. Had she sounded like Hillary? Or was Douglas entirely, completely wrong?

"I'm not like her at all." She managed to keep her tone cold and dignified. "You should know that by now."

His expression told her he had doubts.

She wanted to shake him, and yell, "Douglas! How can you think that?" But all she did was meet his eyes.

And she saw confusion there.

"I wanted . . . I was going to . . ." His voice dwindled.

Douglas looked down. He'd been planning, tonight, to bring up the topic of the future—their future. But Valerie's response to his remarks was causing him to have second thoughts.

He didn't dare make plans—not if there was a chance she really was like Hillary. It wasn't just his own future he had to consider now. It was also the children's. "I think we need a little time to think things over," he said, deciding that sounded reasonable.

She looked crushed.

His hand reached out and he had to make a conscious

effort to pause. He hadn't meant to hurt her, but he was feeling hurt himself.

She sounded so much like Hillary. Had he been wrong about Valerie these last few weeks?

"That's a good idea." Her tone was brittle. She stood up abruptly. "You're right, we need time to—think."

He stood up, wanting badly to reach for her, restraining himself. As he stared at her face, full of emotion—and he recognized she was fighting tears—he wondered if he was making a mistake. Was he wrong?

She handed him his coat, wordlessly, and he shrugged into it.

"I'll call you in a few days," he said, already wishing he hadn't said a word, but had sat on the couch and done nothing but kiss her. Only how would he then know what the true Valerie was like?

"Alright." She said the word stiffly.

In seconds, she had maneuvered him out the door and shut it.

He walked slowly down the stairs, a sinking feeling over-taking his gut.

Had he just blown his whole future?

Chapter Fourteen

Valerie felt upset, and confused over the next few days. She was so glad her class was cooperating and she threw herself into her lessons, class activities, and Halloween preparations.

When they'd baked the cookies at Douglas' home, Valerie had promised Lindsay, at the girl's urging, that she would dress as a princess just like Lindsay this year. The weekend she'd visited her mother she'd picked up the light blue gown she'd worn as a bridesmaid last year for her cousin Abby's wedding, and she had borrowed a cape from Shanna to wear with it. She'd bought a tiara in the costume section of the discount department store, and now that her classroom was loaded with ghost, witch and pumpkin decorations, she was ready.

The teachers' negotiations team met again on Tuesday evening and things went well. The board had sent over a draft of the proposal they were both working on. They spent time refining it, but it looked like things were going exactly as she'd hoped.

If only she felt happier.

Douglas hadn't called, and she hadn't called him either. She guessed he was still thinking. And so was she.

She felt confused and hurt, and unsure about what she wanted to do. She loved Douglas but he had to learn to trust her, she thought again and again.

Wednesday the class' anticipation grew stronger. With Halloween on Friday, they were already so excited it was

172

getting harder for them to pay attention to their work. She was tired and felt some relief by dismissal time.

She dismissed the first group when they were called, and the remaining children, which was less than half the class, settled down. The kids who walked left, and finally the principal was calling the last group when Valerie heard a commotion: "Sir! You can't go there! All visitors have to check in at the office!" It was Shanna, in her most authoritative voice. She had hall duty in their wing of the school today.

Valerie hurried to the door to peer down the hall.

Her mouth dropped open when she saw who was striding rapidly down the hall, with Shanna running after him.

Stuart!

He caught sight of her. "Valerie!" he exclaimed, almost sprinting now.

"Stuart?" she gasped as he slid to a stop by her doorway.

More students were pouring out into the hall now, and casting curious looks their way.

"Do you know this man?" Shanna shouted, unable to keep up with Stuart's long legs.

"What are you doing here? You can't come barging into the school," Valerie declared. Annoyance flamed through her. How could Stuart just show up here, where she worked? And walk down the hall, ignoring all the notices posted in the school requiring visitors to check in at the office? Ignoring Shanna?

Stuart looked older, as handsome as ever, but somehow less reputable than she remembered seeing him. Or was it she had never seen him clearly before?

He grabbed her arm. "I have to talk to you," he snapped. "You can't just brush me off like that. I still love you. I've always loved you!"

Valerie felt her face grow hot as curious students milled around them. She caught sight of Lindsay with two girls from her class. "Stuart," she hissed, shaking off his hand. "Not here!"

Shanna had caught up with them, and now Henry had emerged from his classroom down the hall.

"I'll call the office!" he yelled, and went back to his room.

"Should we call the police?" Shanna asked.

Valerie shook her head. "No. I'll take care of this." She faced Stuart squarely. "This isn't the time or place."

"But babe!" He was whining again.

Valerie heartily doubted that Stuart really loved her. Even now he was too wrapped up in himself. He must have decided he really needed to get married, and for some reason, she fit the bill perfectly.

Henry was back in a moment. He looked at Stuart. "The principal's on his way down."

"Val?" Stuart pleaded.

Anne was rushing down the hall now too. Shanna, seeing Valerie had Anne and Henry with her, rounded up the students and urged them down the hall. "Come on, get to your buses," she directed the kids.

Valerie was vaguely aware of stares, looks of wonder and whispers as the children were shepherded down the hall. With only Anne and Henry hovering nearby, Valerie turned to Stuart: "I thought I made it perfectly clear on the phone," she said, anger making her voice taut. She enunciated each word carefully. "I have no interest in you, Stuart. I don't want to marry you. I don't want to see you." She placed her hands on her hips. "And you should never have come here."

"You're trying to pay me back for breaking up with you, aren't you?" he demanded.

Henry took a step forward. "You have to leave—"

The principal, Mr. Hunt, a usually unflappable man, rounded the corner and came rushing down the hall.

"Here comes the principal," Anne said, her voice grim. "I suggest you listen to Valerie and get out of here quickly."

Stuart cast Mr. Hunt a look, then turned back to Valerie. "You can't mean this—"

"Believe me, I do!" Valerie retorted. Had she really thought she was in love with this man years ago? It must have been a young girl's infatuation. Stuart was utterly self-centered and immature.

"I'm calling the police," Mr. Hunt panted as he slid to a stop next to their group.

If Valerie wasn't so angry, she would be laughing right now. Stuart did look kind of ridiculous as he heard Mr. Hunt's announcement.

"Please leave," Valerie reiterated coldly.

For one moment, she saw shock in Stuart's face. Followed rapidly by anger.

"You'll be sorry. I could have given you a great life," he snapped, turning.

She called after him. "Not the one *I* want."

Douglas was taking Riley for a walk, waiting for the bus to drop off Matthew and Lindsay. The minute the bus rounded the corner, Riley tugged, eager to see the kids and their friends. Lindsay and Matt practically tumbled out of the bus. "Uncle Doug! Uncle Doug!"

He caught their anxiety at once. "What is it?" he asked, as the dog jumped around them and they got tangled in her leash.

He straightened the leash and they walked home together. Apparently, Lindsay had witnessed something distressing, and now she and Matt wanted him to do something.

"This man was telling Valerie he loved her—"

"And Lindsay said they called the principal—"

He had to ask a few pointed questions to sort out their out-of-order tale. They went inside the house, and over juice and the last of the pumpkin muffins, they related what had happened at dismissal from school.

He finally got enough details to realize precisely what was going on.

Some man had shown up at the school, by Valerie's classroom, and proceeded to declare his love for her.

Douglas' stomach plunged down into the basement.

Had he been right? Did Valerie really have another boyfriend?

Did he love her? Did she love him?

But *he* wanted her!

His thoughts ricocheted faster than any ping-pong ball.

A man professing to love Valerie, trying to persuade her, from what the kids were saying, to accept his proposal? Douglas could feel the blood draining away. She couldn't—she wouldn't—

"We want you to do something!" Lindsay declared tearfully. "We want her to marry *you*!"

"Do—what?" Douglas said. But as he said the words, he was fighting an impulse to jump in his car and high-tail it over to Valerie's. To tell her not to accept the other guy. Because—he stopped, staring at the kids.

Because he loved her.

And in that instant, Douglas knew his thoughts were true.

He loved Valerie. He had been falling in love with her all along. And he hadn't even recognized it.

He loved Valerie. It was that simple.

And he'd been that oblivious.

"You can't let her marry this other guy!" Now it was Matt's turn to say his piece. "He's not her type," he said, as if that ended any arguments. "*You* are."

Douglas focused on the children's anxious faces.

"You're absolutely right," he said. "I can't let her marry this other guy. I love her. And," he added, watching the delight spread across their faces, "I think that maybe, she loves me."

"What are you gonna do?" Matt asked.

"I'm going to do something," Douglas said. He needed to take action to prove to Valerie that he really did love her. A plan began to formulate in his mind. "And I might need your help."

Chapter Fifteen

Halloween at school went as smoothly as any holiday could.

The kids were elated, practically jumping with anticipation, and Valerie kept them busy with Halloween word searches, Halloween math puzzles, and other activities geared around the holiday. The weather was cloudy but not cold—perfect for Halloween. The costume parade and classroom party during the afternoon were fun, and afterwards Valerie played the spooky music tape, read a few more stories, and one of the room mothers did a craft project with the children—making witches out of styrofoam cups and balls with pipe cleaner brooms. They ate candy, popcorn, and vegetables with dip, and drank juice. Valerie was proud to note that her students cooperated and everyone got along beautifully.

"I like your costume," Kayla said to Scarlett, shyly. Scarlett was wearing a black cat costume that someone had obviously made for the little girl, and she looked cute.

"Thanks," Scarlett said slowly. She looked at Kayla, who was dressed as little red riding hood. "I like yours too."

And that, Valerie thought, was the best thing that could happen.

She smiled at them both. "You both have great costumes. What kind of candy will you be giving out at your houses?" and they launched into a discussion, joined by Jorge and Amanda, about favorite candy.

Everyone pitched in to clean up, and they were just finishing when the first group of buses was called. "Have fun trick-or-treating! Don't forget to have your parents check your candy!" Valerie said to them as they left.

Shanna, dressed as a cowgirl, waved from down the hall as Valerie watched the children leave.

The incident with Stuart had been a major source of gossip the day before, but with Halloween upon them, the talk had died down this morning and Valerie was hoping that would be the end of it. She certainly expected that that would be the end of any contact with Stuart.

The next group was called a few minutes later. Then the last bus group was called, and Lindsay stopped by Valerie's door. She looked adorable, in a long pink dress and tiara, and Valerie had complimented her and Matt on their costumes.

"Will you be home later?" Lindsay asked.

"Yes," Valerie said. "I have to help the Burtons answer the door and give out candy." Mr. and Mrs. Burton appreciated her helping, since they were both old and got tired of answering the door pretty quickly. And her downstairs neighbor had also asked her to help, since he wouldn't be home from work until late, and he'd given Valerie money for candy.

She wondered if Lindsay and Matt were thinking of trick or treating over at her house. And wondered how she could bear seeing Douglas again, knowing how confused he was feeling.

She tried not to think about it. The room mothers had helped straighten up, so she was able to close up her room swiftly. Since it was Friday, everyone was leaving right away, and in the office the teachers, most of them in costume, were hanging up their keys and departing.

"Have a great weekend!" Ruby, dressed as a female superhero, told her gaily.

"You too," Valerie said, knowing her friend was seeing James again.

Anne, who was dressed like Princess Leia from *Star*

Wars, was equally perky. Valerie tried not to feel disheartened as she left the building, knowing that after Halloween, she had nothing much to look forward to for the weekend.

She barely had time to freshen up at home before the stream of children began to pass by the house. Being on a fairly busy road, they expected to get a number of visitors. The Burtons had already set up a comfortable chair for her in the hallway. Still in costume, Valerie brought the candy she was giving out with her plus a radio and a book to read between trick-or-treaters.

"Just let me know when you get tired and want us to take over," Mrs. Burton told her, handing Valerie a mug of cocoa and a bowl of chocolate bars. "And we have pizza here, so whenever you're hungry we'll heat up slices for you."

"Thanks." Valerie settled in. Turning on the radio, she listened to her favorite female DJ on the local oldies station. After some Halloween talk, she played, "I Put A Spell on You."

Valerie wished she could cast a spell on Douglas.

Instead of reading, she found herself thinking about Douglas. More and more, she was thinking she should call him. She deliberately turned to thoughts of her class. Compromise was working in her classroom. It was working in negotiations—

Maybe she should apply it to love.

Her thoughts were interrupted as children began arriving. The first ones were the youngest kids, out early with their parents, including some toddlers and babies in strollers. But by five o'clock there was a proliferation of the elementary-school-age ghosts, devils, beautiful princesses and superheroes.

Valerie enjoyed seeing the costumes, greeting people from the neighborhood and even a couple of her students who lived nearby. As it got closer to six o'clock, the teens started to come out. Many of the girls wore creative costumes like Dorothy from the *Wizard of Oz*—complete with a small tape recorder that played, "We're off to see the Wizard." Most of the boys were dressed as scary creatures. There was a multitude of ghouls and hatchet-wielding characters from horror films.

There was a lull for a few minutes and Valerie got to sit down and read. She was wondering about having a slice of pizza when someone knocked on the door again.

"Trick-or-treat!" some kids chorused.

Valerie opened the door and found Matthew and Lindsay outside.

"Hi!" she greeted them. "You two look wonderful!" Lindsay looked beautiful in her pink princess costume, and Matthew looked appropriately sinister as a vampire with a black cape and pointy fake teeth. "Pick what kind of candy you want," she told them. "And since you're my friends, take two!"

As they made their selections, she glanced around. Where was Douglas? He wouldn't just drop the kids off and leave them alone, would he? "Where's your—"

"Thank you!" they both declared, as if on cue.

A figure stepped out from the shadows on one side.

Douglas wore jeans and a jacket—and on top of his head, a gaudy gold crown.

He looked comical and Valerie couldn't help it that her heart somersaulted as soon as she saw him. She gave him a look of exaggerated surprise. "Douglas? What are you supposed to be—a king?" Her heart was beating somewhere up in her throat.

He gave her a slow, wide smile, and took her hand. Warmth shot up her arm.

"Not exactly," he said in a commanding voice, bowing over her hand. "I'm a prince. Prince Douglas Cooper, at your service." He straightened, and winked.

A giggle made her turn to look at the kids. They were smiling.

She swiveled to regard Douglas again. His crown was a surprise, and for a moment she simply stared at him. A prince?

"I've come to save the beautiful princess," he said. "You."

"Save me? From what?"

"From—I don't know." He stopped, looked unsure. "From loneliness? It's traditional that princes save princesses."

"Unless the princess knows karate," Valerie responded, remembering their discussion weeks ago. "I don't know karate, Douglas, but I don't need saving." She added the last with some asperity.

She thought Matt snorted.

"I know." Douglas said, then cast the kids a glance. They grinned up at him.

"Okay, time to go back to the car," he told them, pointing his thumb at the curb.

"Can we go next door for candy?" Matt asked.

Douglas looked back at Valerie.

"I know the family," she told him. "They're nice— they'll be okay. And I know the people in the next house down too."

"Alright," he told them.

The kids skipped away, holding their plastic orange pumpkins, already almost-full with candy.

Valerie regarded Douglas silently. He squeezed her hand. Suddenly, his expression was serious, and something in his eyes made her feel like her insides were made of another candy—marshmallows.

"I know you don't need saving," he repeated, shifting his position. "But—this prince wants a happily-ever-after."

"A happily-ever-after?" she asked softly, her heart hammering.

He gazed at her tenderly.

"I want that happily-ever-after with *you*, Valerie," he said, his voice low. "I realize you're not like Hillary.

You're way more special than she could ever hope to be. I want to be with you, to spend my life with you." He lifted her hand and brushed a kiss across it. "I love you, Valerie. And I want to spend the rest of my life loving you."

It seemed like the stars were bursting with happiness, like fireworks were blasting all around them!

"Oh, Douglas." Her breath caught, and she felt tears.

He slid his arms around her waist and kissed her. Waves of happiness rushed through her.

"Please say you share that same dream," he whispered when he released her lips.

"Yes, I do," she said. "I love you, Douglas. I have for— oh, I think since I met you."

"Do you know," he said, his voice a warm rumble, "I think I fell in love with you from the start too. I was just too stupid to realize it." He grinned again. "But I know it now, and I'm never going to let you go. As a matter of fact, if you hadn't said yes, I would have kidnapped you."

"Said yes? You haven't officially asked," she challenged, but the smile she gave him was loving.

He dropped to one knee. "Princess Valerie, will you marry me?" he asked in courtly tones.

She curtsied. "I will, Prince Douglas."

He grabbed her hands again, and laid them on his heart. She could feel his heart beating, hard, beneath his thin jacket. "I love you," he said solemnly. "I hope you realize that—"

Valerie loosened one hand and touched his lips with her trembling fingers. "I know. I was—hoping you loved me, Douglas, but then when you never said it—"

"I didn't realize what this feeling was inside," he admitted. "It took me a while—but I know it now, and I'll always love you, Valerie. And maybe someday we'll have more kids too," he added.

"I'd like that," she whispered.

He stood up and kissed her again.

She heard footsteps coming rapidly up the sidewalk.

There was a delighted giggle, then the children cata-pulted out of the shadows and threw themselves at them.

"Whoa!" Douglas exclaimed.

Valerie and Douglas hugged them back.

"We wanted Uncle Doug to marry you," Lindsay said.

"Yeah, and we told him he better hurry up," Matt said with great authority.

Valerie laughed. "I couldn't think of any children I'd want more than you two."

"Okay, now you really have to give me another minute alone with your Aunt Valerie," Douglas told them. "We have to . . . finish our negotiations."

Shrieking and laughing, the two ran for the car.

"Negotiations?" she asked, raising her eyebrows.

"Negotiations." He kissed her forehead tenderly. "Jessica and Sean are coming over in a little while, so I can come back and spend time with you. Then we can make our plans. I want to marry you soon. I want that happily-ever-after to start right now." He grinned. "I'm willing to com-promise just like the board when necessary."

"So am I," she whispered, touched by his words. "We've negotiated the best agreement of all—love."

"Love," he agreed, and pulled her into his arms for an-other round of negotiations.